Madame Retsmah Predicts

Michael Coleman

**SCHOLASTIC
PRESS**

Scholastic Children's Books,
Commonwealth House, 1-19 New Oxford Street
London WC1A 1NU, UK
a division of Scholastic Ltd
London ~ New York ~Toronto ~Sydney ~ Auckland

First published by Scholastic Ltd, 1998

ISBN 0 590 19714 2

Typeset by DP Photosetting, Aylesbury, Bucks
Printed by Cox and Wyman Ltd, Reading, Berks.

10 9 8 7 6 5 4 3 2 1

Chapter 1

"**F**ogarty, you're a complete and utter simpleton!"

Foggy frowned. This was a bit unfair. Having "Baldo" Baldock calling him names was bad enough, but calling him names he couldn't understand was even worse.

"Er . . . how do you mean, Mr Baldock?"

Baldo ran a hand across his shiny head, uprooting one of his few remaining hairs as he did so. The English teacher looked yet again at the piles of paper towering on all sides of his desk. Then he took a deep breath. Being asked a question by Nigel Archimedes

Fogarty, the doziest boy he'd ever encountered, was a new experience. He wanted his answer to be worthy of the moment.

"Simpleton," he said, glowering across his desk. "A word comprising two parts, Fogarty – 'Simple', meaning a person with cotton wool between his ears, and 'ton', meaning a person with a ton of cotton wool between his ears!"

"Got you," said Foggy, nodding slowly.

Baldo got to his feet, making one of the piles of paper totter.

"When brains were given out, Fogarty, you weren't just at the back of the queue – you turned up on early-closing day!"

Foggy turned all this over in his mind. Nasty names. Baldo in one of his not-so-jolly moods. There was only one conclusion to be drawn.

"Er . . . some sort of problem is there, Mr Baldock?"

"A problem, Fogarty? Dear me, no. Not *a*

problem ... *a thousand* problems!"

Losing the struggle to control himself, Baldo slammed a heavy fist down on one of the paper stalagmites covering his office floor.

"A *thousand*!" bawled Baldo, his face turning purple. "And all because of you, Fogarty!"

Foggy plucked a sheet from the top of the nearest pile. The familiar banner headline leapt out at him:

TERM TIMES
The Newspaper of Lord Turnpike School

"Bottom left-hand corner, Fogarty," said Baldo. "Tell me what you see."

Foggy looked. There, in the bottom left-hand corner of the front page, was his photograph. *His* photograph. With a big cross in the middle of it. Just as he'd expected.

"My spot-the-ball competition picture," said Foggy. "Action scene from last week's First XI football match."

Baldo had stopped pacing. Now he was resting his brow against the cool glass of his office window. It looked like Humpty Dumpty trying to climb a glacier.

"And what did you do?" moaned Baldo.

These questions are getting easier! thought Foggy. He took it slowly, making sure he got things in the right order.

"What did I do? Well, after I took the picture with my polaroid camera I went to the Technology Room and scanned it in to the graphics package on the computer. Then I edited the ball out of the picture. Then I loaded the desk-top publishing system and pasted the ball-less picture file into the space you'd given me on the front page."

Baldo was stunned into momentary silence as he struggled to understand how a blockhead like Fogarty could know so much about computers when he, a man who could quote Shakespeare for England, had to be shown how to turn the thing on.

"The photograph, Fogarty," growled Baldo finally. "Look at the photograph."

Foggy looked at his picture closely. He'd taken it in a bit of hurry. Well, a lot of a hurry to be honest. He'd only had enough time to dash across to the football pitch, take just the one picture, then dash away again. All things considered, he thought, it had come out pretty well.

"Not bad. Nice contrast. Sharp focus." Foggy nodded happily. "Best spot-the-ball picture we've had for ages."

"Fogarty!" roared Mr Baldock. "I'm not talking about the quality of the picture. I'm talking about what's in it!"

He snatched up another, identical, sheet from the pile. "'A spot-the-ball competition,' you suggested. 'Guess where the ball is in this picture. Win a prize of £10.'"

"Right! Good idea, eh?"

Baldo waved the picture furiously under Foggy's nose. "Not when the lunatic with the camera snaps a picture of the school captain taking a penalty kick!"

Foggy looked at his picture once more. A penalty? So that's why all the other players hadn't seemed to be moving around much!

"Oops," he said.

"Oops!" yelled Baldo. "Is that all you can say?" He waved furiously at the stalagmites. "One thousand pupils attend this school, Fogarty. One thousand! And what do you see here? Nine hundred and ninety-nine correct solutions, all claiming their share of the £10 prize!"

Foggy did a bit of mental arithmetic. Not about how much each winner would get, that was a bit on the tricky side. He settled for a simple subtraction.

One thousand, take away nine hundred and ninety-nine, equalled . . . one.

"Somebody got it wrong, though, didn't they, Mr Baldock? So it couldn't have been that easy, could it?"

Baldo slumped back into his chair. "Wrong again, Fogarty. It *was* that easy. The person who got it wrong was the only person in this school who *could* have got it wrong. The only person who could challenge you for the *Simpleton-of-the-Year* title ..."

As if on cue there was a rat-a-tat at Baldo's door, a quick rattle of the knob, and in flew a wild-haired girl.

"Hello, Mr Baldock! Hello, Foggy! Oh, no! Sorree!"

In her haste the girl had bumped into the paper tower nearest the door, sending it toppling on to the pile next to it. Down went the other piles, one after the other like dominoes, until the last of them swamped Baldo's feet in a tide of a-fraction-more-than-a-penny-winning solutions.

"Come in, Edna," he sighed.

"Thanks, Mr Baldock. Ooh. Is that where the ball really was?"

Edna had picked up one of the sheets and was looking at the picture with a cross on the penalty spot.

"It is," said Baldo.

"Boo. I got it wrong."

Baldo closed his eyes. "Yes, Edna, you did. Out of the whole school, you were the only person who didn't realize that Fogarty's picture was of a penalty kick being taken."

"Course I realized it!" retorted Edna. "But then I thought about it a bit more and I thought, come on Edna, I thought, nobody could be that stupid!"

"Do you mind?" said Foggy.

"So I had a guess it was somewhere else," said Edna.

"Balanced between his shoulder blades?" said Baldo, pulling out Edna's losing entry.

"It could have been!" said Edna, indignantly. "Have you ever seen that guy play football? Talk about tricky. I had half a mind to shove my cross up his shirt."

"Half a mind," sighed Baldo. "You never spoke a truer word, Edna. However, I didn't ask you to see me so that we could discuss the dimensions of your mind."

Edna looked at Foggy. Foggy shrugged.

"Dim-what?" said Edna.

"Size," said Baldo. "Or, rather, lack of it. I wanted to see you about this."

He handed Edna a copy of *Term Times*, but this time with the back page uppermost.

"Your recipe," he said wearily. "Read it, if you would."

Edna scanned the page. Her contribution was there, its headline in the bold black box she'd given it.

COKERY COLUMN
by Enda Grice

"Well?" said Baldo.

"Soppy me," said Edna. "You don't spell 'cookery' like that, do you? Me and my typing. I'll get my own name wrong next!"

"You *did* get your own name wrong," said Baldo. "However, I wasn't talking about that, or 'cokery'. Read on."

> This week we are muking custard trats. First, take 500 grims of mustard powder...

Edna looked up. Her eyebrows narrowed. Her bottom lip protruded. "That don't sound right."

"Right?" yelled Baldo. "Of course it doesn't sound right! Because it isn't right! Mustard powder," he scoffed. "Have you got any idea what a tart made with mustard powder would taste like?"

"Not so hot," said Edna.

"Quite the opposite!" shouted Baldo.

"My only consolation is that nobody in the school could possibly have been so stupid as follow your recipe to the letter!"

He got slowly to his feet.

"Three weeks," he muttered. "And then it'll all . . ."

"Sorry?" said Edna.

Baldo shook his head. "Nothing, nothing." He gazed at Edna and Foggy. "Look," he sighed, "I know you both want to do things for the school newspaper. I know you're keen . . ."

"As mustard," said Edna quickly.

Beside her, Foggy said nothing. He seemed lost in thought.

"But," Baldo went on, "I just can't stand any more."

"Then sit down, sir," said Edna.

The English teacher uprooted another couple of hairs. "What I mean, Edna, is that I've had enough. That's it. The end. You've both made your final mark on *Term*

Times..." He quickly placed a hand on the corner of his old oak desk as he added, "...touch wood!"

"Sir!" cried Edna.

"No," said Baldo decisively, "my decision is final. You two half-wits have had your last chance."

Edna glowered. "We are not half-wits! We are not! Are we, Foggy?"

"Er ... what was that?" said Foggy, trance-like.

"Well, anyway, I'm not!" snapped Edna. "Please, Mr Baldock. It won't happen again, I promise. I'll check my typing with a fine toothbrush. It'll be perfect in future..."

"Future?" A sudden, thoughtful, look crossed Baldo's face. He repeated the word again, very softly. "Future..." It was as if Humpty Dumpty was weighing up the pros and cons of jumping off the wall.

"Very well," said Baldo, coming to a

decision. "I'm going to give you pair one more chance."

"Really!" squealed Edna. "Thanks, Mr Baldock!"

"You can work together – and come up with a horoscope column. You do know what a horoscope is, I take it? And don't say a cross between a video nasty and a telescope or I'll brain you."

"I know what a horoscope is," said Edna. "It tells you your future. What the stars hold for you!"

"Correct. And as nobody in their right mind believes that sort of superstitious tosh, you can write any old rubbish and it won't be noticed. All right?"

Edna nodded furiously. "Definite-lee!"

"How about you, Fogarty?"

Foggy's head jerked up, as if he'd been suddenly awakened from a deep sleep. "Er..."

"Good," snapped Baldo. He got to his

feet and began to thread his way between the paper piles. "Now if you two will excuse me, I've got a meeting about the school Summer Fayre with Councillor Daley and Miss Gimlet."

As the teacher shot off down the corridor, Foggy turned to Edna. He looked as if, somewhere inside his head, a wheel had finally stopped revolving.

"You mean..." he said slowly, "that recipe of yours *shouldn't* have said mustard powder?"

"No, of course it shouldn't," said Edna. "Why?"

"Oops."

"Don't tell me you made some!"

Foggy nodded. "This morning, in cookery. Six of them. Came out a treat, they did. Miss Gimlet thought so, too."

"Miss Gimlet?" The mere mention of the name of the school's headteacher was enough to make Edna's blood run cold.

"Just going past the Cookery Room as I came out, she was. Said, 'They look nice, Fogarty.' So I asked her if she'd like one."

"She didn't take one!" cried Edna. "Tell me she didn't take one!"

"She didn't take one..." said Foggy, happy to oblige.

"Coo, thank goodness for that!"

"She took the lot."

"You're joking!"

"Nope. Said they'd go down well at the Summer Fayre meeting she had lined up for this afternoon, she did. Two each for herself, Mr Baldock and Councillor Daley."

Edna started down the corridor. "Two each! One will be enough to put them into orbit! Foggy, we've got to stop..."

She was interrupted by three distant cries of agony – the sort of cries that a head-teacher, an English teacher and a Chair of Governors might make shortly after taking large bites out of custard tarts that had been made with mustard powder.

Foggy spun on his heel. "See you later. I'm going home."

"What about our horoscopes project?"

"That's *why* I'm going home."

"To think about how we can predict the future?"

From the end of the corridor the scream of a steaming, red-tongued Baldo split the air. "Fogar-ty!!!"

"No, because I'm already thinking about it, Edna!" yelled Foggy, breaking into a sprint. "And I'm predicting that if I don't go home now I won't *have* a future!"

Chapter 2

Foggy rattled on the knocker. After a short delay he heard a bolt slide back, then another. A heavy chain clanked. Finally, the door squeaked open by the merest fraction.

"Who is it?" rasped a harsh voice from behind it.

"Me, Foggy. Is that you, Edna?"

"Yes," said the voice. "Now listen. I'm going to count to three, then I'm going to open this door. When I do, you get in here dead slippy. Got that?"

"Three, open door, slippy," repeated

Foggy. Exciting stuff. "Information recorded in the Fogarty personal database," he said. "Ready when you are."

"Right. One – two – three –"

Foggy threw himself forward, smacking his nose hard on the bell-push. The door hadn't moved.

"Four!"

As the door was flung open, Edna's hand shot out and grabbed him by the front of his shirt. Before Foggy knew it he was in the hallway and the door had been slammed shut.

"You said on the count of three!" moaned Foggy, holding his nose with one hand as he felt for his handkerchief with the other.

"I did?" said Edna. Her eyebrows dipped thoughtfully. "You're right. I did. Sorree. DON'T SIT THERE!!"

Foggy, who'd been about to sit on the stairs while he massaged his nose, shot up again, cracking his knee on the banisters.

"Sorree, again," said Edna as Foggy staggered. "Didn't mean to make you jump. STAY WHERE YOU ARE!! DON'T MOVE!!"

"I'm not, I'm not!" squawked Foggy, keeping as still as he could considering his nose was running and his knee was throbbing.

Edna was looking hard at the floor. Surely she wasn't going to ask him to float now?

"What's going on?" said Foggy.

"Retsmah's escaped," said Edna, not lifting her eyes from the floor.

"Uh?"

"My pet. My beautiful. My little coochy-coo. I let her out for her daily run around and the little rascal dashed off while I wasn't looking. Now I can't find her anywhere."

"Ah," said Foggy, feeling just the faintest glimmer of hope that he might not have stumbled into a nut-house.

"You must think I'm dotty," said Edna.

Foggy didn't have time to nod before Edna added, "I just didn't want you treading on her, that's all. She's only little, is Retsmah."

"Retsmah? What sort of name is that?"

"A good name. It's *hamster* spelt backwards."

That figures, thought Foggy. He peered cautiously round the hallway. "Have you tried calling her? Retsmah! Here, Retty, Retty."

Edna put her hands on her hips. "Well *that* won't do any good, will it?"

"Why not?"

"Because she's not out here. I shut her in the kitchen."

Shaking his head in bewilderment, Foggy hobbled after Edna as she tiptoed down the passageway and quietly opened the kitchen door.

"All clear. Come on. And watch where you're treading."

Foggy slid in, pulled a chair away from the small square breakfast table, confirmed that it wasn't already occupied by a small furry thing, and sat down quickly.

A thought suddenly struck him. What did hamsters on the run do? If the beast showed any of the style of his owner then taking refuge up the nearest trouser leg was a definite possibility. Easing his hands down to his ankles, Foggy tucked his trousers into his socks.

"Had any ideas, then?" said Edna, sitting down on the other side of the table. "About the stars?"

"More than an idea," said Foggy, relieved that they were getting down to business at last. "Have a look at this lot." Digging into his jacket pocket, he pulled out a handful of index cards and spread them across the kitchen table.

Edna picked up one of the cards. "Unlucky day: Friday," she read aloud.

"You can say that again. Retsmah always escapes on a Friday. It's as if she knows the weekend's here and she wants to get out and about."

"Here's another one," said Foggy. "Lucky colour: brown."

"Retsmah's brown," said Edna, looking hopefully beneath a dishcloth.

"Really?" said Foggy, yawning. "Well, well, well."

"All right, I can see you don't care!" said Edna. She turned back to the table of index cards. "So what's the big idea?"

"Well," said Foggy briskly, "I've done one card for every day of the week – lucky day Monday, unlucky day Monday, lucky day Tuesday, unlucky day Tuesday and so on – and the same for the numbers from one to nine – lucky number 1, unlucky number 1, lucky number . . ."

"Two, two, the same to you," said Edna. "Come on, get on with it."

"And the same for some colours," said Foggy.

"Yes?"

"Well ... er ... I thought we could pick them out at random. You know, one for each star sign."

"What, like – Scorpio ..."

Edna closed her eyes and whirled her finger in the air before bringing it down on top of one of the cards.

"... Unlucky number: 4."

"Right!"

Edna turned away and fiddled absently with the vegetable rack. "I suppose Retsmah must be a Scorpio."

"Yeh, yeh. And don't tell me, she's got four legs as well."

"No, she hasn't actually," said Edna, looking round the floor again.

Foggy immediately felt bad. A hamster without four legs. Poor thing. No wonder Edna was so worried. What did his own flattened nose and cracked knee matter, anyway?

"So what do you think?" he said gently.

"I think she must be under the fridge."

"About the horoscopes!" yelled Foggy.

"Oh. O-kay, I suppose," shrugged Edna. "But aren't they supposed to say more? You know, like 'your money troubles will soon be over because you're going to break your neck.' That sort of thing?"

Foggy snapped his fingers in triumph. "They most certainly are," he said, digging into his other pocket and pulling out a second pack of cards, "which is why we need these! I found them at the back of my wardrobe."

Edna looked at the cards, at Foggy, then back to the cards once more.

"You must be joking."

"No, I'm not. Definitely not."

Edna took the pack and slowly began to turn the cards over one by one. Each had a brightly coloured picture on it.

"Apple. Bottle. Cat. Dog. Elephant ... Foggy, these are flash cards!"

"I know. Good, eh? Just what we need! We pick one of those at random as well."

"And say what?" said Edna, "'Unlucky animal: elephant'?"

"Of course not!"

"What then? 'You will meet a large grey elephant. Do not stand in its way.' Great. Baldo's going to love that!"

Foggy grabbed the cards back. "No, not that sort of thing. They're for giving us inspiration. Like..." He held up the elephant card "'...big things are in store for you this week!'." He switched to the big red apple card. "'Something embarrassing will happen. Will you go red!' Get it?"

"Clever Foggy!" said Edna, nodding. "So, let's see. If we pick out the kite card, say, we could have ... er ... 'This week you'll be floating on air ...'"

"Precisely!"

"Or. . . 'This week things could really take off for you.' "

"Absolutely!"

"Or, 'This week you'll get your knickers in a twist . . .' "

"Noooo!"

Edna was about to ask why ever not, even Baldo the confirmed bachelor must have heard of knickers, when she suddenly realized that Foggy hadn't been noooo-ing at her. He'd been noooo-ing at something else. Swinging round, she saw the small brown shape eyeing Foggy inquisitively.

"Retsmah! Cherub! You *were* under the fridge!"

"Get away from me!" Foggy screamed as Retsmah started to scuttle his way.

But Edna's pet clearly hadn't been to obedience classes. As Retsmah kept on coming, Foggy took evasive action. Throwing the pack of picture cards in the air he leapt up on to his chair.

"Now look what you've done," yelled Edna as a startled Retsmah turned tail and scuttled back under the fridge. "You've frightened her!"

"I've f-frightened *her*?" stammered Foggy, his eyes glued to the scuttler's hidey-hole. "Wh-what do think *she's* just done to *me*? You said you had a hamster!"

"Indeed I did not," retorted Edna.

"You definitely did," said Foggy. " 'Retsmah,' you said, 'is "hamster" back-wards.' "

"So?" said Edna, hands on hips. "That's what I *was* going to call a hamster if I got one, and get a hamster was what I *was* going to do, but when I got to the shop and saw little Retsmah in her little tank, well, I forgot all about hamsters and got her instead but I still called her Retsmah anyway because that was what I was going to call the hamster I didn't get. Get it?"

As far as Foggy was concerned it didn't matter whether he got it or not. What did matter was what he'd seen. "B-b-but ... that's a ..."

"Scorpion," said Edna, kneeling down to peer beneath the fridge. "Ever so cute, isn't she?"

"B-b-but..." said Foggy, sounding more and more as if he'd developed a fault, "aren't they deadly?"

"Only if they sting you," said Edna. She picked up one of Foggy's fallen cards and waggled it backwards and forwards. "Retsmah! Coo-ee! Come and see!"

From his chair, Foggy was trying to keep one eye on the floor while he looked for possible escape routes with the other. He'd just discarded the notion of leaping on to the draining board and squeezing out through the ventilator when Edna got to her feet again.

"She's not coming out," she sighed. "I

expect she's in a mood, and I can't say I blame her. Having a dirty great pack of cards chucked at you must be really frightening if you're just a diddy little scorpion."

Foggy didn't argue. He didn't move either.

Edna looked up at him. "Are you coming down? We aren't going to get these horoscopes done with you up there doing your lighthouse impersonation, are we?"

Foggy waved a shaky finger at the floor. "Somebody needs to pick the cards up first."

"You," said Edna. "I'll do the writing."

"No, no," said Foggy, trying to sound gentlemanly. "I'll do the writing. I can write standing up. No problem. You pick the cards."

"No, fair do's," said Edna. "You did the cards. *You* can pick them."

Foggy had started to ease himself off his chair when a scratchy, scrabbling sound told him that Retsmah was on the move again.

The appearance of a pair of fierce brown pincers confirmed it. Foggy leapt back to the safety of his chair as the rest of the scorpion emerged and made a beeline for the elephant card.

"Hello, little mate!" cried Edna. She laughed happily. "Like the elephant, do you? Maybe a big thing is coming *your* way!"

"Well I'm not it!" yelled Foggy. "You pick the cards!"

"I know," said Edna brightly as Retsmah scurried across the kitchen floor to inspect another card. "Retsmah can pick them!"

Sweeping the lucky/unlucky cards off the table to join the picture cards that Foggy had scattered in his panic, she spread them out with her foot. Then she handed a pencil and paper up to Foggy. "Whenever Retsmah puts her little tootsies on one, I'll call it out. All you've got to do is write them down."

Slipping to her hands and knees, Edna shuffled across to where Retsmah was sniffing hopefully at the apple card as if she was waiting for a worm to pop out of it.

"Right, elephant was first. Now it's the apple."

Giving up her worm wait in disgust, Retsmah scuttled on. At every stop, Edna called up to Foggy.

"Zebra. Star. Umbrella. Flower. Monkey. Jar. Kite. Watch. Rat." She looked up towards the ceiling. "How many's that? I think Retsmah's little legs are getting tired."

"Eleven," said Foggy. "We need one more."

"Bottle!" yelled Edna as Retsmah made her final port of call. Scooping the scorpion up with a shovel, she dropped it into the glass tank it called home.

"All right, sweetie?" said Edna. "Happy now?"

"Much happier," said Foggy, descending warily to ground level.

"I wasn't talking to you, dumbo!"

snapped Edna. "I was talking to my beautiful Retsmah." Plonking the scorpion's tank down on the table between them, she pulled Foggy's list towards her. "Come on, then. Let's get on with working out what they all mean."

"That . . . she . . . it . . ." stammered Foggy, trying desperately to remember anything they'd ever been told in Biology about a scorpion's glass-eating abilities.

"Retsmah can watch us," said Edna. "After all, she did the choosing." Her eyes lit up. "Hey, *that's* what we can call it!"

"Call what?" said Foggy.

"Our horoscope column. Every newspaper column has to have a title, doesn't it? We can call ours *Retsmah Predicts*. No, no – **Madame** *Retsmah Predicts*! You're a lady, aren't you, cuddle-pops!"

Foggy cast an anxious glance at the scorpion. The thing was scratching the glass wall of its tank as if it was getting itchy feet again.

"We can call it Rumplestiltskin for all I care," he said. "Just so long as we get it done quickly."

"Not bad," said Edna, forty minutes later. "Not bad at all."

Foggy had to agree. It looked good. When the flash cards they'd been working from were rubbed out and the whole thing was typed up it would look even better. Almost professional.

Madame Retsmah Predicts...

Aquarius (Jan 21–Feb 19) – ELEPHANT
A lucky week. Big things are in store for you!
Lucky day: Saturday
Pisces (Feb 20–Mar 20) – APPLE
Something could happen to make you go red.
Unlucky day: Tuesday
Aries (Mar 21–Apr 20) – ZEBRA
Wear stripes this week – they suit you!
Lucky number: 2
Taurus (Apr 21–May 21) – STAR
You will shine all week. Lucky number: 1

> **Gemini** *(May 22–Jun 21) – UMBRELLA*
> *Don't forget your umbrella, you might need it!*
> *Unlucky colour: white*
> **Cancer** *(Jun 22–Jul 23) – FLOWER*
> *A bunch of flowers could be coming your way.*
> *Unlucky day: Wednesday*
> **Leo** *(Jul 24–Aug 23) – MONKEY*
> *Somebody will try to make a monkey out of you.*
> *Unlucky day: Sunday*
> **Virgo** *(Aug 24–Sep 23) – JAR*
> *Something could happen that will leave you in a*
> *jam. Unlucky number: 6*
> **Libra** *(Sep 24–Oct 23) – KITE*
> *This week things could really take off for you.*
> *Unlucky day: Friday*
> **Scorpio** *(Oct 24–Nov 22) – WATCH*
> *Get ready for a really good time. Grab it with both*
> *hands! Lucky colour: blue*
> **Sagittarius** *(Nov 23–Dec 21) – RAT*
> *A person you know will turn out to be a rat.*
> *Unlucky number: 8.*
> **Capricorn** *(Dec 22–Jan 20) – BOTTLE*
> *Don't bottle things up – let it out! Lucky*
> *number: 4*

"You want me to type it up?" said Edna.

Foggy checked the predictions for any mention of custard or mustard. They looked safe enough. Which was more than could be said for the one who'd chosen them. Edna's scorpion was eyeballing him through the glass walls of her tank. Could they high-jump? He wasn't going to wait to find out.

"Fine," said Foggy, heading for the door. "Just make sure you spell-check it, yeah?"

Chapter 3

First thing Monday morning found Edna comfortably settled in front of the English Department's computer.

Like Foggy, computers held no fear for her. She might not be able to type the word accurately in a million years – "copstewer", "composter" and "moptooter" were the best of her recent attempts – but she could use one with her eyes closed.

Some deft slides of the mouse, a few quick clicks, and she was into the school's desktop publishing system. Another couple of clicks and up came the blank outline for that week's edition of *Term Times*.

Zooming in on the back page, Edna quickly found what she was looking for. A large, empty box with a double-line border had been set aside for them to fill. "Stars: Fogarty and Grice" read the temporary heading.

"Stars!" cooed Edna. "That's what we'll be when this lot comes out!"

Just so long as her typing didn't let her down again, she then told herself. She leant over the keyboard, her tongue sticking out in concentration. Her typing *wasn't* going to let her down! Not this time. This time her typing was going to be as accurate as that William Tell geezer shooting the apple off his son's head. Oh, yes. This time Baldo wasn't going to have a reason to get the pip with her!

Slowly Edna replaced the temporary heading, over-typing it with their own.

MADAME RETSMAH PREDICTS

Perfect. Dipping into her bag, she pulled out the sheet of horoscopes she and Foggy had devised from the results of Retsmah's walkabout. With renewed confidence, she typed the first line.

> AQUARIUM (January 21–February 19)

"Oh, boo!" said Edna as she looked up at the screen and saw what she'd just typed. "I ask you – aquarium! What are you, Edna?"

"A big wet Nellie?" growled a voice from behind her.

Edna didn't have to turn round to see who it was. Reflected in the bottom of her screen, Baldo's head looked like the morning sun peeping over the horizon.

"Hello, Mr Baldock. We've done our horoscope column. I've just started to type it."

"Just started to tripe it, more like," said

Baldo. He bent low to peer at the heading. "Madame Retsmah Predicts," he read. "Retsmah? Miss Grice, I can't even *guess* what that word's supposed to be."

"That *is* what it's supposed to be," said Edna. "It's 'hamster' backwards and she's a girl and she helped me and Foggy a lot so we called it after her. See?"

Baldo didn't say, one way or the other. He just scowled as he said, "Just make sure it's done by lunch-time, eh? Miss Gimlet likes all the contributions in before she does her bit. The pest."

"Pardon, Mr Baldock?"

"The best, I mean," said Baldo hastily. "The best. Save the best till last."

Edna nodded. Miss Gimlet's regular piece, "Head Lines", always took prime position on the front page. In the past, issues of *Term Times* had been delayed until it had been written.

"Deadlines," said Edna solemnly.

"Head Lines," said Baldo. "Her column's called *Head Lines*."

"No, deadlines," repeated Edna. "I know about them. If we don't do our bits by our deadline then Miss Gimlet can't do her bit by her deadline and Councillor Daley can't arrange the printing ..."

"Don't you worry about the printing," said Baldo, his tone softening as if it had been mixed with some magic ingredient in a washing machine, "Councillor Daley won't let us down. You just get that column done."

"Yes, Mr Baldock."

The English teacher went to leave, then paused. "Out of interest," he said, "what are you predicting for Cancer the crab?"

Edna hastily covered the page of predictions with her hand. What was the first rule of journalism? Reporters never revealed their tomato sauces. Something like that. If Baldo thought she was going to reveal what Retsmah's little pincers had predicted for his birth-sign then he was very much mistaken.

"I'm afraid I'm not at liberty to say," she said, before throwing in a dose of sales-talk for good measure. "Get your *Term Times* on Wednesday and read all about it!"

As Baldo sniffed, muttered something about "who cares?" and stalked off, Edna turned back to her list and checked the entry for Aquarius. "A lucky week. Big things are in store for you." She'd just typed:

> A yucky week. Bog things are in
> stir for you.

when the door rattled open again.

"Not another recipe, I trust," said a voice with more icicles hanging from it than a frozen gutter.

Edna turned and smiled nervously. "No, Miss Gimlet. A horoscope."

"With the accent on the horror, no doubt," said the skinny headteacher.

Framed in the doorway, she looked like a pencil in a box. "Talking of which," she added, as the temperature of her voice plunged several degrees lower, "if Councillor Daley should wander in here, can you please try to answer her questions sensibly..."

Miss Gimlet paused as if she'd just remembered who she was talking to. "Well, as sensibly as possible," she sighed. "It seems our chair of Governors isn't satisfied with spending half her life in the school. She actually wants to know what goes on here as well."

"You can rely on me, Miss Gimlet," said Edna brightly. "I'll show her what a good thinker I am."

"That's what I'm afraid of, Edna. So if in doubt, say nothing. Got that?"

"Say nothing. Got it, Miss Gimlet."

Giving the impression that she doubted if Edna Grice had ever got anything except

German Measles, the headteacher closed the door. Suddenly it opened again as she looked round it and asked: "By the way, what do you predict for Cancer?"

Another one! thought Edna. First Baldo, now Miss Gimlet. Were crabs naturally nosy? Or was she being tested?

Of course, she was being tested! Her headteacher had deliberately asked her a trick question, one she knew that Edna wouldn't be sure how to answer.

Well, she'd show her! What had Miss Gimlet herself just said? *Edna, if in doubt, say...*

"Nothing, Miss Gimlet," said Edna.

Councillor Daley arrived just as Edna reached the very entry that Baldo and Miss Gimlet had asked about.

CONKER (Junk 22–Jelly 21)

Like a perfumed whirlwind, the Chair of Governors blew through the door and into the room. Pulling up a chair, she plonked herself down next to Edna.

"And you are?" beamed Councillor Daley.

Edna thought about the question. Tricky or not? She turned it over in her mind as warily as if it were the crust of a school dinner pie. A safe one, she decided finally.

"A girl," said Edna confidently.

"Name, dear."

Still safe, reckoned Edna. "Councillor Winifred Daley."

"Not *my* name, dear. Your name!"

"Ah. Edna."

Councillor Daley gave a relieved, but satisfied, nod. "And what are you doing, Edna?"

No problem again. Miss Gimlet had nothing to worry about here! "I'm talking to you, Councillor Daley."

"What I meant was," said the Councillor slowly, "what were you doing before you started talking to me?"

"Nothing," said Edna.

It had been the only possible answer. For all she knew, Councillor Daley could be anti-horoscopes. She might be anti-computers. She might even be anti-girls-doing-typing-because-they-shouldn't-get-it-into-their-heads-that-they-have-to-be-secretaries-because-they-can-be-undertakers-deep-sea-divers-anything-they-want-to-be-especially-County-Councillors.

Councillor Daley's beam was showing clear signs of battery failure. "Of course you were doing something," she said, "you were typing! What were you typing?"

Back on safe ground, thought Edna with relief. "Keys."

"You mean horoscopes!" Councillor Daley jabbed a finger at Edna's screen. "I can see that's what you were typing! For the school newspaper, no doubt."

There was no way of denying it. "Horoscopes, school newspaper," echoed Edna. "Yes."

Councillor Daley's eyes narrowed, like those of a dangerous snake. "Mr Baldock mentioned something about a horoscope column at our Friday meeting," she spat. "After we'd recovered from eating tarts some lunatic had made by following another lunatic's recipe."

Then, as suddenly as she'd turned nasty, Councillor Daley switched her headlights on again. "A wonderful innovation, the school newspaper. A wonderful innovation by a wonderful headteacher. So, tell me. What will *Term Times* be predicting for, say, Cancer the crab?"

"Nothing," said Edna, again.

"Nothing?" squeaked Councillor Daley, rising from her chair in frustration. "Nothing? How can you have a horoscope with nothing as a prediction?"

"Easy. I haven't typed it in yet."

"All done, Foggy," said Edna as they met in the dining hall at lunch-time. "I typed in our horoscopes, *and* spell-checked them, so there'll be no mustards instead of custards this time!"

"Good stuff," said Foggy.

"Good?" sniffed Edna. "It was gooder than good. I thought I'd never get them finished, I was interrupted so many times."

She went on to tell him about her conversations with Baldo, Miss Gimlet and Councillor Daley. "But they didn't get anything out of me," she finished. "I kept Dad."

"Interesting, though," said Foggy thoughtfully. "So all three of them are Cancer, are they?"

Edna looked at him. "How'd you work that out?"

"Stands to reason, don't it? You don't ask about somebody else's star sign, do you?"

"You might," said Edna. "Maybe Mrs Baldo is a crab. Maybe he wanted to know so that he could tell her."

Foggy shook his head. "There isn't a Mrs Baldo. There was a profile of him in the first edition of *Term Times*, remember? It said he lived with his mum and fourteen cats. So unless he was wondering about one of the cats, it's got to be that Baldo's a Can-..."

He stopped as a quite amazing idea shot between his ears. At the same instant, Edna gave a little screech of excitement.

"I have just had the most amazing thought," said Foggy.

"Coo!" said Edna. "So have I. I was just thinking what a whizzo thing it would be ..."

"If one of Retsmah's predictions..." continued Foggy, lowering his voice.

"Came true," murmured Edna, from behind her hand.

"Because we *made* it come true," hissed Foggy.

"Yes!" whispered Edna. "Great minds think alike, Foggy!"

Foggy wasn't sure just how much he wanted his mind bracketed with that of Edna Grice, but there was no doubt about it. The idea they'd both had was a belter.

"But whose horoscope should it be?" said Foggy.

They'd settled for a low murmur after discovering that neither of them was much good at lip reading.

"Baldo!" suggested Edna. "If his horoscope came true he couldn't possibly take us off *Term Times*, could he?"

"How about Miss Gimlet?" countered Foggy. "She's Baldo's boss, isn't she?"

"How about Councillor Daley?" counter-countered Edna. She's Chairbody of the Governors. Doesn't that make her Miss Gimlet's boss?"

"Er ... I suppose it does," said Foggy. "You think she should be the one, then?"

"Definitely," said Edna firmly. "Or Miss Gimlet."

"Or Baldo."

"There's only one way to decide this," said Edna.

She pulled the salt and pepper shakers across the table. Then, plonking the vinegar bottle in between them, she began. "Ip-dip-dip, my-little-ship..."

It must have been the sight of the three items lined up together that gave Foggy his second sizzling idea in as many minutes.

"Why not all *three* of them?" he said. "If they're all Cancer then a perfect horoscope shouldn't just come true for one of them, should it?"

"You're right! It should come true for all of them!"

Dipping in her school bag, Edna pulled out the sheet of predictions. "Here we are.

Cancer. 'A bunch of flowers could be coming your way. Unlucky day: Wednesday.' The day *Term Times* comes out."

Foggy chuckled. "No problem! What d'you reckon, partner? Is a bunch of flowers each a good idea, or what?"

"Foggy," said Edna, "it's a blooming marvellous idea!"

Chapter 4

Foggy chose red roses. It was an unwise choice. As he remembered the moment he shoved the three bunches inside his school jumper to keep them out of sight, roses have thorns.

Racing indoors again he heaved on his thickest anorak, placed the prickly bunches outside his jumper but inside the coat, zipped it right up to his chin, then set off to meet Edna at the school gates.

"So what did you get?" asked Edna as he panted across the road fifteen minutes later.

"Roses," winced Foggy.

"Not hydrangeas – a hardy flowering shrub with opposite leaves requiring a rich loam soil which should be well-drained but not dry? Or hyssop – a hardy blue-flowered plant with stems which are shrubby near the ground but herbaceous above?"

"No, roses," said Foggy, impressed at Edna's knowledge of horticulture. "They were all I could find in our garden."

"Need to be kept in the warm, do they?" she asked, as Foggy wiped his sweating brow.

"Of course not. This is a security device."

"Looks like an anorak to me."

"A security anorak, then. There's no point Baldo and Co. seeing us turn up with flowers, is there? They'll know we've fixed things. We want them to believe Madame Retsmah's prediction has come true."

"Smart thinking," said Edna. "Maybe I should wear one too." Ferreting in her seemingly bottomless school bag, she pulled out a plastic raincoat and put it on. "You want to give me a bunch to carry?"

Foggy shook his head. "Not really. That's a see-through coat, Edna."

"Silly me, so it is," giggled Edna. "Tell you what, I'll lead the way. First stop, Miss Gimlet ..."

Miss Gimlet's office was at the end of the main corridor of the White House.

This large, whitewashed building was the administrative heart of Lord Turnpike School. Lessons were held in the tall concrete and glass monstrosities that had sprung up after the estate was acquired, but the White House was different. Located slap-bang in the middle of the extensive school grounds, it had originally been the home of Lord Turnpike himself.

Foggy and Edna slipped through the double doors and into the White House lobby. On either side of them the two halves of the double staircase swept to the first floor balcony. Between them, and hanging just beneath the balcony railings, a portrait of Lord Turnpike gazed down at them. Foggy returned the gaze, as he always did when he came this way. Having been called totally bonkers himself on a number of occasions, he always liked to have a look at the genuine article.

For totally, completely and utterly bonkers was what Lord Turnpike certainly had been. How else could you describe a man who thought he was a mole, and dug tunnels everywhere to prove it? It was rumoured that there were dozens of the things beneath the school playing fields.

Whatever the truth of that, by Foggy's reckoning there had to be at least one of them somewhere because it was part of recorded history that Lord Turnpike had met his end digging it. He'd starved to death after accidentally losing his bearings and burrowing downwards instead of upwards.

"If we leave them outside her door," whispered Edna, as they headed on down the corridor, "she'll see them the minute she comes out."

Miss Gimlet was an early starter. Foggy and Edna had no doubt that she'd be in her room already. That was part of the plan.

A cloud crossed Edna's face. "Ooh. What if she treads on them?"

Foggy winced as a thorn pierced his school jumper and dug into his ribs. "Then she'd better be wearing army boots. Come on, let's get this over and done with. These thorns are killing me."

Edna stopped, her head moving from side to side. "Here, what's that noise?" A strange snorting sound was coming from some-where.

"I don't know. Maybe they haven't killed today's school dinner yet." Foggy scuttled ahead. "Does it matter?"

Before Edna had a chance to answer,

Foggy discovered that, yes, it did matter. For, just as he reached Miss Gimlet's study and was putting a hand inside his anorak to retrieve her bunch of roses, the door was yanked open.

"Fogardy! Mid Gride!" roared Miss Gimlet at once. "Wha-wha-whaa-choooo!!"

Mystery solved. The snorting had actually been Miss Gimlet sneezing. Her eyes were red, her nose was redder, and two large tears were streaming down her cheeks. She looked like a beetroot onion.

"Wob do you two wod? Oh, I don't care whad you want, jusd go away! And ged rid of these while you're ad id! I'b allergic to dem. Dey make me sneede, and sneede and sneede. And if I find oud who pud them id my room I will skin 'em alive! A-chooo!"

Miss Gimlet went to thrust what she was holding into Foggy's arms until she saw that for some reason he was doing an impression of Napoleon and had his hand jammed inside his coat. Launching them towards Edna instead, she slammed her door shut. From behind it, the sneezing continued non-stop.

"Well I never!" said Edna, putting her nose to what had just landed in her arms.

Foggy stared, open-mouthed. He'd never either. Never thought for a minute that *this* would happen. That very morning Miss Gimlet had received, and now just thrown away, an enormous bouquet of flowers.

Their prediction had actually come true!

"Brilliant," said Foggy as they left the White House. "We start off with three bunches of flowers, visit our first customer, and what happens? We end up with four instead of two."

Edna may have been uncertain about the arithmetic, but one thing had definitely sunk in. "Retsmah's prediction came true though, didn't it?"

"Coincidence," said Foggy. "Nothing more than that. Let's carry on with the plan."

"Next stop Councillor Daley, you mean? Okey-dokey. We can give her two bunches of flowers. Or three. Whatever you've got in there." Edna pointed at the front of Foggy's anorak. Now hiding Miss Gimlet's cast-off bouquet as well as the roses, it was starting to look as if he'd borrowed it from a sumo wrestler.

Councillor Daley's movements on Wednesdays were well known. Unlike her Monday visits, during which she annoyed the pupils, Wednesdays were devoted to annoying the teachers. Arriving early, she would park her car in its reserved spot behind the kitchens then set up camp in the White House staff room until morning break.

"We can leave them on the bonnet of her car," said Edna.

"Like it!" gurgled Foggy. "Then her bonnet will match her hat."

Councillor Daley's taste in headgear was equally well known. It was awful. She went in for creations that looked like miniature gardens.

"You what?" said Edna.

"Flowered hat – flowered bonnet. Get it?"

"No."

Neither, as it transpired, did Councillor Daley.

Turning left out of the White House, Foggy and Edna ambled casually towards the back of the building before turning sharp left again and scooting quickly into the secluded parking area reserved exclusively for teachers and nosy governors.

Councillor Daley's swish saloon was in its usual spot. Ducking low so as not to be spotted, they scuttled across to it. This time, both their mouths fell open.

"That is *unreal*," cried Edna.

The inside of Councillor Daley's car was festooned with flowers. They'd been beaten to it again.

"Unreal is right, Edna," said Foggy, pressing his nose to the windscreen and examining one of the flowers. "They're silk flowers. In fact, they look just like the sort Councillor Daley has on her..."

"Hat!" giggled Edna.

"Right again," said Foggy, impressed.

"Flowered hat, flowered bonnet! I get it! Funny, Foggy. Really funny!"

But Foggy wasn't listening. He'd gone to the back of the car and was looking in through the rear window.

"They *are* off her hat," said Foggy. "Look!"

The remains of Councillor Daley's hat were on the parcel shelf. Someone had given it a severe pruning.

Edna inspected the evidence for herself. It was quite, quite conclusive.

"Retsmah, you clever thing," she said admiringly. "You've done it again. No, you've double done it!"

"Double done it?" Foggy frowned. "What are you on about, Edna?"

"The prediction, of course. 'Cancer. A bunch of flowers could be coming your way...'"

"Yes, yes."

"And '*Unlucky* day, Wednesday. Today's Wednesday, Foggy. And that hat looks pretty unlucky to me!"

"Edna," insisted Foggy as they hurried away from Councillor Daley's car, "there is no way you're the proud owner of a fortune-telling scorpion."

"I wouldn't be so sure about that," replied Edna with a shake of her head. "She's got two out of two so far. I think she could be."

Foggy hurried on. He had a more immediate problem. With ten minutes to go to registration, he still hadn't got rid of a single bouquet.

"I'd prefer to think about these," he said, irritably patting the front of his bulging anorak. "What am I going to do with them, open a flower stall?"

No sooner had he spoken than he saw the solution to his problem hurrying towards the White House. It was a tall, very bald solution, and was carrying a pile of paper under its arm.

"Baldo!" hissed Foggy. "We can go back to Plan One and give them all to him!"

Edna stuck a thumb in the air. "Good thinking. Quick, let's have them. You can leave this to me."

With an immense sigh of relief, Foggy pulled out Miss Gimlet's rejected bouquet, followed by the bunches of roses. He handed them over to Edna. "How are you going to do it," he whispered, "sneak them up to his office?"

"Nope."

"Hide them in the staff room?"

"Nope."

"How, then?"

"Easy," said Edna. "Watch."

She stepped out, straight into Baldo's path. "Hello, Mr Baldock. We've got some flowers for you!"

Baldo slithered to a halt. "Flowers? For me, Miss Grice? But – why?"

"To say sorry for us getting our *Term Times* pieces all wrong last week, not to mention the mustard tarts..."

"Do *not* mention the mustard tarts."

"I won't. And also to say how we hope we'll do better this week with our horoscopes..."

Baldo's eyebrows rose, like a pair of caterpillars doing press-ups. "Your horoscopes?"

"That's right, sir. Course, we don't know what sign you are, do we Foggy, but if it should happen to be Cancer, well now, that would be absolutely a-mazing, because I remember our Cancer prediction being something to do with a bunch of flowers coming your way which would mean we'd got it spot on and, come on Mr Baldock you couldn't chuck us off the paper if we were good enough to do that, could you. . ."

Baldo held up a hand. "Miss Grice. Do I look as if I was born yesterday?"

"Definitely not, Mr Baldock!" said Edna.

"Good."

"Because yesterday was June the seventh. That would make you a Gemini and Geminis weren't down for flowers."

Slowly, Baldo eased the flowers from Edna's fingers. Then, rather more quickly, he tossed them into a nearby waste-bin.

"What I mean, Miss Grice, is that unlike you two, I'm not a mug." He smiled, reminding Foggy of a nature programme he'd once watched about how cracks appear in glaciers. "I've also seen your horoscope column."

Baldo plucked one of the sheets from the pile under his arm and handed it over. It was the latest edition of *Term Times*. "Your typing seems to have let you down again, Miss Grice."

"My typing?" muttered Edna as Baldo stalked off towards the White House. "What's he on about?"

Foggy's finger did the talking. He pointed to the entry for Cancer.

CANCER (June 22–July 23)
A bunch of flour could be coming your way.
Unlucky day: Wednesday

"A bunch of flour?" yelled Foggy.

"But . . . I checked it. I'm sure I did."

"Edna, I've spent the whole morning feeling like a pin cushion and for what? Nothing! Because I shouldn't have had roses up my jumper, I should have had bags of flour! Why didn't you say so? I could have called in at the supermarket and wheeled it here in a trolley..."

Foggy might well have ranted on for some time if the crash hadn't interrupted him. Coming from the entrance to the White House, it sounded like the sort of noise something heavy might make if it were to land on somebody's head.

It was – because it had. On Baldo's head.

Racing across, they saw the English teacher staggering about beneath the portrait of Lord Turnpike. He was holding the top of his head and moaning loudly.

Foggy gasped. "I don't believe it!"

Baldo looked as if he'd seen a ghost. Correction, he looked *like* a ghost. His head and shoulders were covered in white. The tattered remnants of a large brown bag dangled from the top corner of Lord Turnpike's picture frame.

"Flour bombed," breathed Foggy. "Edna, he's been flour bombed!"

Beside him, Edna cooed with delight. " 'A bunch of flour could be coming your way!' Retsmah, you clever thing, you!"

Chapter 5

"What a week!"

Foggy slumped on to the chair furthest from Retsmah's glass cabinet.

Edna went over and peered through the glass. "She's having a little snooze. I'm not surprised. All that brain-work must have been dead tiring for her."

"Come on, Edna. You don't really believe old pincer-paws over there is a fortune-teller?"

"I don't know, Foggy. It's a bit weird, isn't it? Dead mysterious."

"Baldo didn't think there was any mystery

about it, did he?" exclaimed Foggy. "He thought he knew who the culprits were, didn't he? Us!"

It had been a painful interview. Baldo had dragged them off to his room and made them wait while he recovered – a recovery that was helped dramatically by his gulping down a good dose of brandy from a bottle he plucked from his filing cabinet.

Then, his head still looking like a cream bun that had lost its cherry, Baldo had started yelling.

"You two arranged that!" he yelled. "Admit it! You rigged that sack of flour up, to make your prediction come true!"

"You're wrong, sir," Foggy had said. "We didn't know Edna had made a typing mistake. That's why you got the flowers."

Baldo turned on Edna. "A likely story. Those flowers were just a decoy."

"No, they weren't," said Edna defiantly, "they were roses."

"Don't try to put me off the scent, Miss Grice," snarled Baldo. "That bag could have done me a nasty injury. I was lucky it caught on the frame of Lord Turnpike's picture and split open. If it had hit me on the head, I wouldn't have got up in a hurry."

Edna looked unconvinced. "You might have. The bag said it was self-raising flour."

That was the moment, with Baldo looking as though he was about to do something to them that he wouldn't regret later, when Foggy had decided to come clean about what they'd been up to.

"It couldn't have been us, Mr Baldock. We were in the car park."

"In the car park?"

The voice came from the corridor outside. At the sound of it, Baldo's attitude changed at once.

Brushing himself down as he muttered, "I can't let her see me like this," he impatiently shooed Foggy and Edna from the room.

It had been like jumping from the frying pan into the fire. The voice, as they'd immediately discovered, had been that of Councillor Daley. Emerging from the Staff Room, she'd overheard their debate with Baldo. Seeing them, she'd repeated her question.

"In the car park?"

"Yes, Councillor Daley," said Edna.

"Near my car?"

"Yes."

"And my hat?"

"Three in a row," said Edna. "Don't they call that a hat-trick?"

Councillor Daley hadn't answered, one way or the other. She'd simply expanded with rage and roared, "You took a pair of garden shears to my best hat, didn't you!"

"No!" cried Foggy. "It was already done. "We were . . . er . . . going to *give* you a bunch of flowers."

"That's right," said Edna. "We had a

bunch for you, and a bunch for Miss Gimlet. . ."

As if on cue, the headteacher had swept down the corridor at that very moment.

"Flowers for me! A-choo!" she sneezed. "Knowing full well, a-choo, I'm allergic to flowers, a-choo, a-choo! So you two planted them in my office, did you?"

"No, Miss Gimlet!" said Foggy.

Edna added her logic to the argument. "Foggy's telling the truth, Miss Gimlet. We didn't plant them in your office. I mean, you saw us, remember? We didn't have forks with us, did we?"

As Miss Gimlet gave a soft moan, Councillor Daley pitched in with a question of her own.

"So where are they, then? These two bunches of flowers?"

"We gave them to Mr Baldock. Just before he got clobbered by the flour bomb."

Amazingly, this new piece of information

had terminated the discussion.

A soft glow had lit up at the back of Miss Gimlet's red and puffy eyes. She'd murmured, "A flour bomb?" And then, without a further word, had hurried off in the direction of Baldo's room.

Councillor Daley, on the other hand, had simply snapped, "Flour bomb? What that man needs is a bomb *under* him, not on top!" She'd then stormed off back to the Staff Room, leaving them alone.

And that had been the end of the matter. No more discussion – and no suggestion, whenever they'd since bumped into Baldo, that they shouldn't produce their predictions for the coming week's *Term Times*.

So, thought Foggy as he spread the flash cards across the kitchen floor, could Retsmah do it again?

Over in the corner of the kitchen, Edna had been tip-tapping a welcome on the scorpion's glass tank with her fingernail. As the creature finally twitched one pincer she beamed in delight.

"Look, Foggy! She wants to help us again. Isn't that right, Retsmah? You want to make some more of your brilliant predictions?"

The scorpion scuttled out from its hiding place – to Edna, as clear a sign of agreement as if it had opened its jaws and croaked, "You bet!"

"This is just a game," said Foggy as Edna let Retsmah loose a couple of minutes later. "You do agree, there's no way that . . . thing . . . can predict the future?"

"Of course she can't," said Edna. "I mean, some of the others were way out, weren't they?"

And some! thought Foggy, judging from the reports that had filtered through to them.

The school secretary, birth-sign Libra, was supposed to be facing a week that "would really take off". So how come the fire brigade had needed to be called to the tower block she lived in to rescue her from a lift?

And how come Melanie Fleet in Foggy's Science group, a Scorpio who should have been ready to grab a good time "with both hands", had fallen asleep with boredom, slipped off her stool, and broken her arm?

And how come Rupert Goodbody in the top Maths group, an Aquarian for whom Retsmah had predicted that "big things were in store" had been discovered by the school nurse not only to have an IQ of 164 but nits as well?

"No, I agree," said Edna. "Little Retsmah can't tell everybody's fortune." She bent down to look her pet squarely in the eyes. "Maybe you can only do it for Cancer-ites, like Baldo, Miss Gimlet and Councillor Daley. Is that right, sweetie?"

"Edna..." groaned Foggy.

"And why not?" said Edna. "Cancer is the sign of the crab, isn't it? And crabs have pincers, just like Retsmah's got. That means crabs and scorpions must be related."

"So?"

"So that could be how Retsmah can tell their fortunes. She's mentally telepathetic, or whatever it is." She bent to give the scorpion an encouraging smile. "Come on then, my little mate. We'll start with Cancer."

Encouraged or not, Retsmah immediately perked up. It looked one way, then the other, as if it was waiting to cross the road. Suddenly it scuttled forward, only to stop with its left pincer on one card, its right on another.

"Two cards is no good," said Foggy. "We want one."

"Maybe she can't make up her mind," said Edna. "Or – hey, maybe she's telling us she wants both. Yes, that's it."

"In that case," said Foggy, looking down at the picture under Retsmah's left pincer, "we have an envelope ..."

"And ink," said Edna, easing Retsmah's right pincer up with a teaspoon to confirm that the flash card beneath it definitely did picture a bottle of the stuff.

"So what can that give us?" said Foggy.

Edna stared at Retsmah as if trying to work out what would have been going on between the scorpion's ears if it had had any.

"How about: 'You will be opening an envelope ... er ... when you get covered in ink'?"

"No!" yelled Foggy. Having Baldo turned into a lump of puff pastry had been bad enough. Predicting that he'd become a walking blot was asking for trouble.

"Maybe Retsmah has got something nice and peaceful in mind," he said, "like: 'A letter will come your way'."

Edna looked doubtful. "What about the ink, then? If Retsmah wants ink, then ink she's got to have."

"Letters are written with ink, aren't they?" said Foggy. "Doesn't that cover it?"

Edna's sniff told Foggy that no, it didn't

cover it. He racked his brains. What was needed was a crafty way of fitting the word "ink" into Retsmah's prediction, but in a way which wouldn't tempt the fates to send gallons of it flying in all directions.

Edna bent down and gave Retsmah a motherly tickle. "Lovey-dovey," she cooed, "what did you think when you picked ink?"

Ink – think! Perfect! Foggy leapt on the idea at once.

"I've got it! Instead of mentioning ink, we can use a word that's got ink as part of it."

"I don't know..."

Foggy pointed at Retsmah, who was still cuddling the flash card. "Look, she's only got part of her pincer on it, hasn't she? That must mean that 'ink' only forms parts of whatever she's thinking of. Yeah?"

It was an argument with a dottiness level worthy of Edna herself – and it worked.

"All right," she nodded. "So what's the prediction?"

"Well," said Foggy, "something like: 'A letter will come your way. It will make you ... er ... something-ink' "

"Clink?" suggested Edna.

"Think! 'A letter will come your way. It will make you think!' "

Foggy congratulated himself. He couldn't believe for a minute that Retsmah was clairvoyant, even for Cancerians and other close relatives. But, *if* she was, then at least the prediction he'd just come up with would give them a trouble-free week.

Foggy was in the school library when the copies of *Term Times* arrived, hot off Councillor Daley's printing presses, the following Wednesday lunch-time.

He snatched one and was about to turn to the back page when the bold leading article caught his eye.

> ## WIN A MILLION!
>
> Yes, it could be you-hoo! Thanks to the persuasive powers of Miss Gimlet, Mr Baldock and Councillor Daley, the greatest-ever prize could be won at this year's Summer Fayre. An insurance company has agreed to offer the sum of
>
> ### £1,000,000
>
> to anybody who can hit a golf ball straight into a hole one hundred metres away – otherwise known as a "hole in one". The odds against achieving this are phenomenal, but at £1 a go it must be worth a try!
>
> As a further temptation, the money itself will be on display! Yes, securely contained in a glass cabinet and guarded by six burly members of the Police Marching Band (who will themselves be an attraction at 4pm!) it will be your chance to see one million pounds in the flesh!

Foggy flipped over to the back page. Yes, there it was. *Madame Retsmah Predicts.* Eagerly he scanned the column. *Not bad*, he thought. *Not bad at all.* Edna's typing was really improving. He couldn't find a single spelling mis—

"Edna, you noodle. You great big noodle!"

As Foggy let rip, the girl herself peered out from behind the encyclopaedia shelf.

"Hysteria, Foggy. That is hysteria."

"What?" cried Foggy.

"A form of neurosis in which organic illness is simulated for some gain."

Edna shoved the fat volume back and plonked herself down beside him. "Good one, eh? It's my new campaign to improve my general knowledge. I look up a new word every day and try to use it. Last week I used hydrangea and hyssop. Yesterday it was hysteria."

"I'll give you hysteria!" Foggy yelled, dropping his voice to a wild hiss as the Librarian gave him an oy-shut-your-noise glare. "Look at that!"

Edna peered down at the horoscope entry for Cancer:

> **CANCER** (June 22–July 23)
> A letter will come your way. It will make you **ink.

"Ooh. Where did that come from?"

"Where do you think? You typed it. Starstar-ink! What's Baldo going to say when he sees that?"

"What's Retsmah going to say when *she* sees it?" grumbled Edna. "Boo. It's not fair. I checked and checked and checked that lot."

Leaving Edna to sulk, Foggy meandered outside for a walk. He had a wide choice of routes. The loopy Lord Turnpike may have spent a lot of time digging underground but it was clear to Foggy that he'd also found time to organize things up top as well. Gravel pathways wandered hither and thither amongst beds of this, that and the other.

Turning right, he began to follow the path which ran directly beneath the library building – only to find himself following Baldo.

Ahead of them both, a ladder was leaning against the wall. Foggy watched as Baldo approached it. The obvious move would have been to walk beneath it, since to go round it meant stepping into a flower bed.

Surely he's not superstitious, thought Foggy. But apparently Baldo was just that. Instead of walking beneath the ladder, he stopped to think about it.

Foggy looked up. Was there a painter dangling from the top, he wondered. No, there wasn't. The ladder ended beneath an open window. But the same thought had clearly entered Baldo's mind. The teacher was looking up at the open window too.

And so it was that they both had a very clear view of the large object which suddenly shot out from this window and couldn't have plummeted more accurately for Baldo's head if the teacher had had a target painted on it.

For a big man, Baldo's reaction was swift. Seeing the object coming towards him he dived for safety – and almost managed it. His top half disappeared into the flower bed, but his bottom half didn't quite make it. With a terrific thump the large object struck his backside.

"Should be all right in a couple of days," said the ambulance driver as Foggy watched them loading Baldo aboard some fifteen minutes later. "Probably keep him in for twenty-four hours' observation, then let him go."

"Ugh!" whispered Edna, coming up behind him. "Fancy observing Baldo's botty for twenty-four hours!"

But Foggy wasn't listening. Miss Gimlet, who'd been on the scene almost as soon as the accident happened, had just retrieved from the flower bed the large object responsible for Baldo's injury.

"Encyclopaedia, eh?" said the ambulance driver. "Not exactly light reading!"

Miss Gimlet glared at him. Then, tucking the hefty volume under her arm, she stalked off past Foggy and Edna. The encyclopaedia's spine was clearly visible as she went by.

Foggy saw it. "Volume 'I' " he said.

Edna saw it, differently. "Retsmah was right again then," she said.

Foggy stared at her. "Edna! The prediction said a letter would be coming his way, not a socking great encyclopaedia!"

"I know. And what's an 'I' if it isn't a letter?"

She was right. She was definitely right! "I never thought of *that* sort of letter," breathed Foggy.

"Well, clever little Retsmah must have. And if star-star-ink made any sense, I bet that would fit, too."

Foggy almost staggered as the flash came. "It *does* make sense," he said. "You know when you're using a word processor to search for a word? You can use a star to stand for any letter you like. So..."

"Star-star-ink means anything-anything-ink?" said Edna. She sucked her thumb thoughtfully. "Like ... er ... what?"

"Blink!" said Foggy. It had to be!

"It will make you blink?" said Edna. "It didn't hit him on the head, Foggy!"

"No, I know. But what it did do was shoot out of that window so fast he didn't have time to get out of the way."

"So, so, so?" said Edna, baffled.

"So you could say it was on him ... in the blink of an 'I'..."

Chapter 6

"Any sign of Baldo?" said Foggy next morning.

Edna took her head out of the giant bag from which she'd been taking sandwiches ever since they left and looked round the coach. "Can't see him."

"Not here," said Foggy. "I meant at school."

Edna shook her head. "He wouldn't have come on this anyway. He's English and sewage farms are Science. Aren't they?"

Foggy said that's what he'd have thought.

"So why's Councillor Daley here, then?" he added.

At the front of the coach, the Chair of Governors was seated next to Miss Gimlet. The headteacher, from the smell wafting their way, was munching honey sandwiches.

"Who knows? Maybe her printing company has something to do with the sewage business."

"How?"

"I don't know," said Foggy. "Maybe they print 'Now Wash Your Hands' on the toilet rolls."

The visit to Butt's Sewage Farm hadn't exactly set the Science Group alight with excitement when it had been announced. But it had to be better than working, thought Foggy. He wasn't to be disappointed.

As the coach scrunched to a halt, a man in a billowing white coat stepped out to meet them. Minutes later the group were being ushered into a large room with control panels and large dials on the walls.

"Good morning," said White Coat, "and welcome to Butt's Sewage Processing Plant. Here we use a number of interesting techniques, in particular the natural use of the activated sludge process in which sewage is mixed with a complex culture of micro-organisms before being dried on open drying beds. . ."

On he went until, some half-an-hour's detailed explanation later, he finally paused for breath and said, "Any questions?"

Edna put her hand up. "There was a bit I didn't understand."

The man in the white coat smiled. "And which bit was that, dear?"

"The bit after 'Good morning'."

Miss Gimlet stepped quickly forward, clearly anxious to keep the visit down to the morning allocated to it. "Perhaps if we look outside?" she suggested. "Miss Grice can see for herself, then."

"Good thinking," said Councillor Daley, striding towards the exit. "This way, is it?"

The class shuffled outside in a crocodile. Up at the front, Councillor Daley's latest hat stood out like a beacon. The vandalizing of her previous one clearly hadn't changed her preferences. This latest version was a flower spotter's paradise, with buds and blooms of every shape and colour jostling for attention.

Miss Gimlet had taken up her position at the back of the crocodile. Between them stood Foggy and Edna and the rest of their class, all holding their noses and generally trying not to breathe.

"Phor!" said Foggy. "What a hum!"

"I can't hear anything," said Edna.

"I didn't mean..." began Foggy, until Edna suddenly looked into the air and said, "Oh, yes I can."

Foggy listened hard. Edna was right. There *was* a humming sound, and it was getting closer and louder. No it wasn't, it was getting further away again.

"There you go," pointed Edna. "It's a bumble-bee."

It was, too. A huge specimen, that had flown over their heads and was now making a very rapid beeline for something further forward. Exactly what, they realized moments later when Councillor Daley's screech of terror rent the air.

"It's after her hat!" cried Foggy. "It must think it's made of *real* flowers!"

At the front of the crocodile, the Chair of Governors was certainly acting as if she had a bee in her bonnet. Whipping her hat off, she tried to whisk the thing away. No good. Back came the bee, causing Councillor Daley to back off too.

"Watch out!" yelled White Coat.

"If she isn't careful," said Foggy as Councillor Daley began running round in circles, "she's going to fall in that..."

The splash stopped him.

"So *that's* a sludge pit!" said Edna. "Nasty!"

In her panic, Councillor Daley had backed too far. As though walking the plank backwards, she'd suddenly disappeared off the pathway and tumbled headlong into . . . well, Foggy didn't want to think what into.

And he didn't have to. For another thought elbowed everything else out of the way.

"The prediction," he breathed. " 'A letter will be coming your way.' It just has – for Councillor Daley!"

Edna frowned. "Bumble? That's not a letter, is it?"

"Not 'bumble'," said Foggy. " 'B'! As in 'bee'!"

"You mean Retsmah got it right again? She is a fortune-teller, then. I knew it!"

A star-reading scorpion? Never. And yet, Foggy couldn't deny that the evidence was piling up in front of his eyes; or rather, in

Councillor Daley's case, in front of his nose.

Even as he watched, the man in the white coat was in the process of hauling the Chair of Governors out of his precious sludge with a long pole. A very long pole indeed.

"Stand back!" he yelled. "She is going to pong to high heaven when she comes out!"

Foggy didn't doubt that. For it was part of the mounting evidence, he'd realized. Star-star-ink had come true for Councillor Daley, too. The full message flashed through his mind as clearly as if it had been in neon lights.

"A bee will be coming your way. It will make you *stink*!"

"I think there's something about this whole business that smells," said Foggy at break time the next morning. "And I don't just mean Councillor Daley."

"What do you mean, then?" said Edna.

"I mean smell as in dead fishy."

"Well of course dead fish smell, Foggy! Anybody could tell you that."

"No, dead fishy as in susfishious – I mean, suspicious. Think about it, Edna. Last week it was flowers – and flour bombs. This week it's letters."

"Just like Retsmah said! I told you, Foggy. She's the scorchingest scorpion that ever . . . er, scorped."

Wondering briefly whether Edna's word-searching had taken her into volume "S" already, Foggy continued. "OK, just supposing she can tell the future. That still doesn't explain how these things happened, does it? I mean, who flour-bombed Baldo? And who tried to brain him with an encyclopaedia?"

"Don't forget Councillor Daley's hat," said Edna, nodding seriously. "Who did that, if it wasn't us?" She looked at Foggy. "It wasn't us, was it?"

"Of course it wasn't! But it must have

been somebody – right?"

"Right. And I know who."

"You do? Who?"

"Retsmah, of course. Once she's predicted something will happen, then that's it. It happens. Fate cannot be denied!"

"You what?"

"Inevitability it's called. That's my word for today. It means if something's going to happen, it's going to happen. So if Retsmah looks into the future and sees something's going to happen then it is and it does and it has. I think. . ."

Foggy thought about it more himself during the next lesson. But by the time came for them to troop in to the Main Hall for the regular Friday Assembly, he was no nearer a conclusion. He'd come up with a theory, though.

"What if there's a pattern?" he said to Edna as they lined up. "This letters business, for instance. Baldo was hit by an 'I', right?

And Councillor Daley was attacked by a 'B'. So if we could work out what might happen to Miss Gimlet, we'd have a chance of stopping it."

Edna shook her head. "Fate cannot be denied. If it's in the stars then ... er ... the sky's the limit."

Their teachers began to file past them and climb on to the raised platform at the far end of the hall. Baldo, moving slowly, and with an unusually large bulge in the seat of his trousers, was amongst them.

Foggy stuck to his guns. "What could the next letter be? Why don't we go through the alphabet?"

Edna sighed. "All right. How about ... 'A'?"

"How? What on earth's an 'A'?"

"Nothing, silly. What I mean is, maybe Miss Gimlet's going to get a whack on the ear and she'll have to go round saying 'Eh? What's that? Eh?' to everybody."

Most of the staff were on the platform now. From along the corridor, the sharp clicking of Miss Gimlet's heels on the wooden floor told them that the lady herself was coming.

"What about 'C'?" hissed Foggy. "As in the sea. Maybe she's going to get hit by a tidal wave." He brightened at the thought. "There's no way we could get accused of making that happen!"

"It could be 'Q'," said Edna. "Retsmah might have seen her getting crushed to bits in a rioting queue. Y'know, like at the January sales."

"Edna. It's the middle of June."

"The June-uary sales, then! I don't know!"

As Miss Gimlet drew near, and their own queue fell silent, Foggy wondered if Edna could be half right. Might the whole school be planning a riot that only they hadn't heard about? Was Miss Gimlet about to be pulverized by a queue of her very own pupils?

The thought disappeared as the head-teacher spoke to Edna.

"Miss Grice. I've forgotten my thermos flask. It's in my room. Would you run across to the White House and fetch it please?"

It was an order, not a question. Without waiting for an answer, Miss Gimlet marched on into the hall and took her place on the platform. It was the signal for the pupils to begin filing in.

But Foggy stood still, allowing others to flow round him like a river round a rock. What if. . .

He grabbed Edna's arm. "Don't get it!"

"Why ever not?" said Edna. "Miss Gimlet always takes her flask into assemblies, you know she does."

"Because that could be the letter! 'T' as in cup of tea! The prediction could be 'Some tea will be coming your way. It will make you drink'!".

"So, what's wrong with that?"

"Er . . . nothing."

Prising herself free, Edna dashed off to Miss Gimlet's room. Foggy, meanwhile, continued to examine the question from all angles. Drinking tea might not be dangerous in itself, but . . . what if it wasn't tea? What if Miss Gimlet's favourite beverage had been doctored in some way?

"Check it, Edna!" he cried as, moments later, Edna raced back with the head-teacher's flask in her hands.

"Why?"

"If it's tea in there. . ."

Edna unscrewed the cap and sniffed. She shook her head. "It's not tea," she said. "So there you go."

Foggy heaved a sigh of relief. It must be coffee. That was OK. Only tea could possibly fit the prediction, and if it wasn't that then all was well. He waited until Edna had handed the thermos flask up to Miss Gimlet, then together they pushed their way through to a couple of spare chairs in the middle of the hall.

On the platform, Miss Gimlet unscrewed her flask. Beneath her a class of first-formers acted out a short play in which a London bus ran round in circles while the rest of them jumped up and down waving swords.

Pour, sip, pour, sip.

By the time the performance had finished, so had Miss Gimlet. While everybody else applauded, she looked forlornly into the bottom of what was now obviously an empty flask.

"What was that all about?" hissed Edna as the first-formers shuffled back into their places. "Road safety?"

"Air pollution," said Foggy. "The bus was causing it and the swords were cutting the hole in the ozone layer."

"Better to have wheeled in Councillor Daley. That would have said it all."

Foggy had to agree. When finally fished out from the sludge tank, Councillor Daley must have done more damage to the quality of the air than a dozen London buses.

"Looks like she's still recovering," said Foggy. Councillor Daley was a regular attendee for assemblies, not being able to resist the opportunity of making a little speech, but today there was no sign of her.

As the applause for the pollution performance died down, Miss Gimlet took a last lingering look into her flask. Holding it to her lips, she tipped it back. A single drip came out, to be swallowed with a loud smack. Only then did the headteacher move forward to the front of the stage and begin to speak.

"There are shome points I swish to bring to your atten ... er ... atten-*shun*!"

All around her, the teachers leapt to their feet. Some even saluted. Miss Gimlet looked confused for a moment, then broke into a fit of the giggles.

"Shilly me. I didn't mean to say that at all! It just shlipped out. Shtand at ease, everybody."

Edna looked at Foggy. "What's the matter with her? She looks as if she's..."

"Drunk!" gasped Foggy. "The prediction! 'It will make you drink.' That's not far off from 'It will make you drunk'!"

And drunk Miss Gimlet certainly was. Tottering to the front of the platform she carried on with what she had to say.

"I want to remind you all about the biggesht runnymazing, no, no, money-raising event in the shchool year."

She swayed forward, then backwards, then sideways before continuing. "It takes place, of courshe, in a fawn-tight, I mean a torn-fight, no, no I mean..."

"A fortnight," hissed the padded-bottomed Baldo from behind her.

"That ish what I shaid, dear Mr Baldy-clock. A floor-newt. Oh, in two weeksh time!

I refer to the Shummer Fayre!"

There could only be one possible explanation, realized Foggy. That flask *had* been laced with some strong drink. But how? And what had coffee got to do with any letter of the alphabet?

Up on the platform, Miss Gimlet was getting excited. "I want to remind you to remind every-booby – parentsh, auntiesh and carbuncles – all about it! Espeshaialilly the chance to win one million smackeroonies as exploded in my article in the news-nutter. Nude-blotter. Newsletter!"

Tottering wildly, Miss Gimlet reached the final point of her speech.

"There will be shtacks going on!" she cried. "Shide-slows everywhere! No, that'sh dot bright."

Miss Gimlet concentrated for all she was worth. Her brain wanted to say "sideshows" but her mouth didn't seem able to do the trick.

"Slide-shows. Snide-snows. Shade-shears. Shine-shoes..."

"Side-shows!" bellowed Baldo from behind her.

It was the final straw – or, as Miss Gimlet would have said if she could have managed it, the final shtraw.

Clearly aiming to pierce Baldo with her fiercest glare, she swung round angrily. The sudden movement proved too much. She lost her balance completely.

Looking like a dagger in flight, Miss Gimlet dived off the platform and into the middle of a sea of first-form swords. Her final act before slipping into unconsciousness was to lift her head and gurgle a quick chorus of "Soup, soup, glorious soup".

"Soup?" said Foggy in the middle of the uproar which followed. "That flask contained coffee didn't it? That's what you said."

Edna shook her head firmly. "No I did

not! You asked if there was tea in it, and I said no, because there *wasn't* tea in it."

"Then you're saying there was soup in it?"

"Yep. But it wasn't alphabet soup, if that's what you're thinking, because I looked. I'm not dumb, you know."

Foggy's mind span. That's exactly what he *had* been thinking. In that case there was no way it could have fitted the prediction. Unless. . .

"Edna. Could you tell what flavour soup it was?"

"Yep. Pea."

"Pea! Pea soup! Pea as in the letter that comes after 'O' and before 'Q'?"

"Yep . . . Ooh, I get it! The letter 'P'!" She shook her head and sighed. "Would you believe it? Retsmah, I've got to hand it to you. You are the greatest."

"Hand it to Retsmah, my foot," said Foggy. "There's something going on here, and we'd better get to the bottom of it fast!"

Chapter 7

"Baldo, Miss Gimlet and Councillor Daley," said Foggy. "Why should somebody have got it in for them?"

"Because they're all horrible?" suggested Edna, tucking into a sandwich of unknown content.

"True," admitted Foggy. "But is that a good enough reason to try and pop them off?"

"Pop them off?"

Foggy nodded. He'd been thinking about what *might* have resulted, rather than what had *actually* happened.

"If that encyclopaedia had hit Baldo on the nut instead of the butt, he'd have been laid out for weeks. And if Councillor Daley hadn't been fished out of that sludge pit, she'd have been a goner."

"Down the plughole, you mean?" said Edna. "You're not wrong, Foggy."

"As it is, she'll be back in action next week, so Baldo reckons. He's expecting her to cause a bit of a stink about what happened."

"How about Miss Gimlet, then?"

"Falling off that platform could have been the end of her, too. Those first-formers were all holding swords, remember. If she'd crash-landed on to one of those she'd have been in worse trouble than Councillor Daley."

"How come?"

"Pronged instead of ponged."

Edna moved on to the second layer of her sandwich box. Mayonnaise had dripped through and mingled with the fairy cakes.

"Fate cannot be denied," she said, tucking in with relish. "If it's in the stars then that's where it is. It's going to happen."

Foggy wasn't convinced. "Edna, that's six accidents! Two each! Is that suspicious?"

Edna looked at her mayonnaise cake. "Yes, it is," she said. "Absolutely suspicious. Wanna bit?"

"Suspicious!" said Foggy. "Not delicious! I was talking about the accidents."

"What about them?"

"What if they weren't accidents? What if they were caused deliberately?"

Edna wrinkled her nose. "How?" she said. "How could somebody have made Councillor Daley-dozen take a dip in the sludge-pit? You were there. That bee caused it." Her eyes opened wide. "You don't think that bee's behind it all, do you?"

"No, of course not. But say somebody planned it? Say they had that bee in a jar or something, knowing full well when they let it out the only flowers it'd see would be that bunch on Councillor Daley's head?"

"Then it would have to be somebody in our group," said Edna.

"Right," said Foggy. "Or ... Miss Gimlet. Hey, she was eating honey sandwiches on the coach. Maybe it was home-made. Maybe she keeps bees!"

As quickly as he suggested it, Foggy shook his head. "No, it can't be her. She wouldn't have laced her own soup, would she?"

"No chance." Edna shook her head solemnly. "She'd have known straight away if she had. Her shoes would have fallen off."

"Edna," said Foggy despairingly, "you don't lace a drink with shoe-laces, you do it with something like gin, or vodka or ... brandy!"

The image of Baldo's brandy bottle, plucked by the English teacher from his filing cabinet in the aftermath of the flour bombing, flashed before Foggy's eyes.

"Baldo's brandy! He could have done it!"

Once again, though, Foggy immediately realized that his theory didn't hold water. "No, Baldo can't be the one doing this. He could hardly have aimed an encyclopaedia at his own head, could he?"

"I don't know. He could have balanced it carefully, then run downstairs ever so fast before it dropped."

"Why?"

"Simple," said Edna. "To make everybody think he didn't do the others because he did this."

"Edna! He could have killed himself."

"Double smart! Talk about a perfect alibi!"

Foggy leapt to his feet. "Baldo can't possibly be a suspect anyway," he yelled, "because he couldn't have been Councillor

111

Daley's bee smuggler. He wasn't on the sewage farm outing, remember? He was in hospital with his bum in a sling!"

"It could have been a remote control bee. He could have been lying there with a handset..."

Foggy let out a low moan. He couldn't take any more. Was this girl naturally stupid or did she take lessons? Leaving Edna to babble on, he staggered outside in dire need of some fresh air to clear his head.

Strolling along the gravel driveway, he rounded the White House and headed towards the car park and the spot where Councillor Daley's car had been the morning he and Edna had paid it a visit.

It reminded him of the other set of mysteries. How had they been beaten to the punch with the first set of predictions, the flower bunch, the predictions they'd tried to make come true?

They?

The thought stopped Foggy in his tracks. It hadn't been *their* idea, it had been his. But Edna had agreed to it without a murmur. Why? Could it have been because she'd been thinking along the same lines too?

And what if she was *still* thinking along the same lines? Foggy ran through the evidence. And the more he ran through it, the stickier it looked for a certain E. Grice.

1 – Councillor Daley's bee attack. Edna had been there. Could she have been the bee-bringer? Perfectly possible. There'd have been room for a dozen jam-jars in that giant bag she'd brought, and as for actually owning one – why, anybody daft enough to keep a scorpion as a pet could have a whole army of creepy, crawly, buzzing things tucked away somewhere.

2 – Miss Gimlet's pea-souper. Who had been the last person to lay hands on the thermos flask? Edna! And wasn't Baldo's room just down the corridor from Miss

Gimlet's? It wouldn't have taken her two ticks to slop in a good measure from Baldo's brandy bottle.

3 – And then there was the flying encyclopaedia. Could she have been responsible? Had he, or had he not, left her in the library looking up her word of the day? Her word of the day . . . Foggy ran through the list. Hyacinth, Hyssop, Hysteria – and what was latest? Inevitability. The significance hit Foggy at once. At the time of the encyclopaedia attack, Edna would have been just about ready to start on volume "I"!

The more he thought about it, the more the evidence built up.

Edna had been waiting for him at the school gates when he'd turned up with the flowers. He'd assumed she'd just arrived. But what was to say she hadn't arrived early, crept to the White House, delivered the flowers that had set off Miss Gimlet's allergy, chopped up Councillor Daley's hat, planted

Baldo's flour bomb, all before coming out again to meet him?

In fact, what had been the first disaster to hit Baldo, Miss Gimlet and Councillor Daley? Edna's mustard tart recipe that he, Foggy, had thought was genuine! Talk about cooking up trouble!

Oh yes, Foggy could see it all now. Edna was carrying out a vendetta. This dimbo-act of hers was just that – an act, brilliantly executed. She'd fooled them all. But no longer.

Edna Grice, he told himself, *your wicked scheme is doomed to failure. You have met your match. From this moment on, I will be watching you like a cork. Yes, indeedy. Wherever you go, whatever you do, Nigel Archimedes Fogarty will be bobbing up and down somewhere!*

"You coming round, Foggy?"

At the sound of Edna's voice, Foggy's eyes narrowed. He gave the telephone a suspicious stare. "Why?" he said.

"Because it's Saturday, and Retsmah's jumping up and down like a mad thing. She wants to get out and make her predictions for next week, I know she does. So are you coming round or do you want me to do them on my own?"

On your own! Not likely!

"I'm on my way," said Foggy icily.

Edna was sitting on the kitchen floor, the flash cards already spread out before her. Retsmah's glass tank was at her left hand. As Foggy came in he could have sworn the creature looked up and gave him a black look. Retsmah stared at him too.

"All ready, I see," said Foggy.

"More than ready," replied Edna. "Retsmah's little pincers have been twitching like crazy ever since I called you. She can't wait to get going."

And, as the scorpion was tipped out of its tank, it seemed as if Edna was right. Retsmah scuttled around the floor like a mad thing. It was as much as Foggy could do to keep up as Edna reeled off the cards Retsmah sniffed at, or trampled on.

"Aquarius – Frog and Monday. Probably means they'll feel jumpy all day, d'you reckon?" Retsmah scuttled on. "Pisces – Strawberry and Unlucky Colour Blue. Well, it would be if you ate a blue strawberry, wouldn't it? Aries. . ."

Foggy jotted down the details, but his mind was leaping ahead to the birth-sign he knew they were both waiting for.

"Cancer," said Edna finally. She looked up, a strange gleam in her eye. "Let's see what Retsmah's got in store for them this week!"

Foggy looked down at the floor. The scorpion was poised in between a group of cards, as if it was trying to make its mind up which disaster to forecast next.

Or was it Edna who was trying to make *her*

mind up? Foggy wondered. Maybe she'd been cheating all along, doing something to make Retsmah move the way she wanted. How did stage magicians manage to make tennis balls whizz about in the air? Black cotton, wasn't it? Foggy peered hard at Edna's fingers. Nothing. At least there was one sneaky trick she hadn't cottoned on to!

"Good girl!" said Edna as Retsmah finally came to a decision and edged one ugly pincer on to a day card. Foggy saw it as Edna said it. "Unlucky day: Saturday!"

"Saturday?" gulped Foggy.

"Summer Fayre day," said Edna ominously. "I hope it isn't going to rain."

If the past couple of weeks were anything to go by, thought Foggy, Baldo for one would gladly settle for nothing more than a drop of rain landing on his head.

Retsmah moved again. Across the floor she scampered, towards a flash card with a big black cloud on it. Foggy's hopes rose.

Surely even the meanest Edna couldn't turn a raindrop into a disaster for Cancereans?

"Oo-er! Nasty," said Edna.

Retsmah had had second thoughts. With a pirouette that would have done justice to a ballerina, she'd spun away from the rain cloud and positively leapt on to the worst card in the whole pack.

"S for Skeleton," said Edna. "What do you reckon that means? Something to do with broken bones?"

Foggy didn't want to think about it. The possibilities of any skeleton-related prediction for Baldo, Councillor Daley and Miss Gimlet were too horrible to contemplate. Baldo being trapped in the coconut shy and his nut being used for target practice... Miss Gimlet and Councillor Daley falling beneath the rhythmic boots of the Police Marching Band... The maniac! He had to stop her!

"No, Edna," stammered Foggy. "I think it means ... er ... something else."

"Really?" said Edna, with what sounded to Foggy like a giggle of evil anticipation. "What, something *worse* than broken bones?"

"No!" cried Foggy. "Let me think, now. A skeleton is sort of . . . under the surface. . ."

Edna snapped her fingers. "That's it! They're going to get buried alive at the Summer Fayre! Like old Lord Toothpick or whatever his name was. There's going to be a JCB digger demonstration, I'm sure there is."

"I didn't mean that sort of under the surface!" gurgled Foggy hastily. I meant . . . er. . ."

What could he say? He had to come up with something completely innocuous; something that even the devious Edna couldn't turn into a life-threatening attempt.

"What I meant," Foggy continued, "was that . . . er . . . we've all got skeletons, and they're sort of ... under the surface of everybody's skin. Which means that ... er ... when you see a skeleton ... you can't actually tell who it is. . ."

"*Was*," said Edna with a look which sent a chill up Foggy's spine. "That's the important thing about skeletons. They're dead. You don't meet them rattling around when they're alive."

Death! This was getting worse! Foggy set off on another mental ramble.

"What I mean is ... if you *did* meet a skeleton you wouldn't know who it was, because it would be like meeting somebody you'd never met before. A stranger. . ."

Even as he said the word, Foggy's heart was leaping in relief. It was the answer he'd been searching for.

"Yes, that's what Retsmah must be predicting. 'You are going to meet a stranger at the Summer Fayre!' "

"A stranger?" said Edna. "Is that all?"

It's worked! thought Foggy exultantly. *She looks sick!* "Yep. That's all. A stranger."

"Well, OK. You write it down, and I'll type it in tomorrow."

Oh, no, you won't! thought Foggy. He wasn't going to fall for that one either! Edna's diabolical typing was also part of her cunning strategy, he'd realized that too – a clever way of explaining how their previous predictions had turned out differently.

If he let her loose on this one, who could tell how it would end up? Probably something like: "You will meet somebody *stronger* at the Summer Fayre." Talk about a racing certainty for a few broken bones!

"How about if I type them up this time?" said Foggy with an air of innocence.

Edna looked offended. "I don't mind typing them. I like typing them. It beats me how the others come out all wrong."

Cool, thought Foggy, *very cool.* He was

going to have to suggest something that wouldn't arouse her suspicions.

"Tell you what. How about if we *both* do the typing."

"Both of us? One finger each, you mean?"

"No," said Foggy. "You can type, while I watch."

And let's see you try anything on with Hawkeye Fogarty looking over your shoulder!

Nothing did happen. Edna didn't try anything – well, nothing that Foggy didn't spot and correct.

"Ah-ah!" he said as she typed, "Unlicky day."

No unpleasant accidents with dogs or ice-cream cornets, thank you very much!

"And again," he said when instead of "Saturday" Edna typed "Batterday".

There were going to be no teachers, headteachers or governors having close encounters with Police Band truncheons – or ending up wrapped in newspaper at the fish-and-chip stall.

"Close," said Foggy as Edna keyed in one more flawed attempt. His knowledge of saints was by no means comprehensive, but if "You will meet St Ranger at the Summer Fayre" was Edna's way of predicting an unscheduled arrival in heaven, then he'd stopped her again.

"OK now?" snapped Edna, finally.

"Perfect," said Foggy, looking at the screen. Nothing could have been clearer or more error-free.

> **CANCER** (June 22–July 23)
> Unlucky day: Saturday. You will meet a stranger at the Summer Fayre.

He'd done it!

Foggy the Fantastic had foiled Edna the Avenger!

If only Baldo, Miss Gimlet and Councillor Daley knew how much they owed him they'd make him *Term Times'* Chief Investigative Reporter and give him the whole of the front page for his exclusive story.

In the mean time he would have to take comfort in knowing that this week, at least, he could predict that *Madame Retsmah Predicts* . . . was going to contain no unpredictable predictions.

And take comfort in that knowledge Foggy did.

Until, on the following Wednesday, he picked up a still-warm copy of *Term Times* and read:

CANCER (June 22–July 23)
Unlucky day: Saturday. You will meet a *strangler* at the Summer Fayre.

Chapter 8

"You will meet a strangler at the Summer Fayre." Nervously, Foggy clutched at his own throat. A strangler! How on earth had she managed to change it?

He was sure he'd seen Edna save her file, then log off. After that, the process was as smooth as Baldo's head. At lunch-time the file would be locked by Baldo himself. After that, nobody could add a thing to it.

Well, almost nobody. Only Miss Gimlet was allowed to add her *Head Lines* piece, during the afternoon. This was supposed to be so that she could have a look at what was in the issue and comment accordingly. What it really meant was that any articles entitled "101 Reasons Why Miss Gimlet Should Go" could be removed and the author suspended before the day was out.

After that the final copy was put on disk for Councillor Daley to take to the printing firm of which she was managing director on Tuesday. There, a thousand copies of the newspaper would be churned out ready for her to bring in to the school on Wednesday morning.

So there was only one explanation. How she'd managed it Foggy didn't know, because they were in the same bottom group for every subject on Monday mornings, but somehow Edna must have come back and altered that prediction.

" 'You will meet a strangler'," breathed Foggy.

What dreadful deed was the fiendess planning?

At that moment, Edna was placing, not planning – placing her copy of *Term Times* flat against the glass wall of Retsmah's tank.

"Look, Retsmah! Look what it's come out as! Read it for yourself. 'You will meet a strangler at the Summer Fayre'! A strangler!"

The scorpion peeped out from beneath its rock, inspected the words briefly, then popped back in again.

"Now how did that happen?" said Edna. "I typed 'stranger', I must have. Foggy was looking at the screen so closely he steamed it up. He'd have said if I'd made a mistake like that."

Or would he? The thought made her draw closer to Retsmah's tank so that she couldn't be overheard by anyone else.

"I've just thought, Retty. What if he wanted me to type something like that? In fact . . . what if he came back to the computer later and changed it himself? In double fact

... what if he changed the other ones as well?"

Retsmah gave a twitch that Edna assumed could only mean agreement.

"I mean, I was sure I'd checked your ink-y prediction that went all wrong. And the flowery one. Hey, maybe Foggy changed them as well!"

Scribble, scrabble.

"You think so too, eh? But why? What's he up to? Because the more I think about it, up to something is definitely what he is. Did you see the funny looks he was giving you when you were doing your stuff the other day?"

Scrape, scratch.

"And who talked me into the 'stranger' prediction? He did!"

Snuffle, sniffle.

"In treble fact, now I think of it, Foggy's been on the scene whenever anything's gone wrong. Yes! He was at the sewage farm – and anybody who can shove three bunches of roses up his jumper could have sneaked a diddy bumble-bee in there with no trouble!''

Twitch.

"And he was first on the scene after Baldo had been beaned with that encyclopaedia. Retsmah, I'm wondering if maybe it didn't fall from that library window. I'm wondering if Foggy was hiding in the bushes with it and leapt out and whacked him! And do you know why I'm wondering that? Because I couldn't find that 'I' volume when I looked for it after he marched off.''

Twitch, twitch.

"Miss Gimlet's soup? Good question, darling. He didn't want me to go and get it, did he? Maybe because he'd already tonked it up with brandy and he didn't want to take the chance of me finding out!''

Two brown pincers clacked together.

"You can applaud, my girl! I've rumbled him, haven't I? He must have got there early and set up those flower happenings. And don't forget the mustard tarts. I know I got the recipe wrong, but who actually *made* them, and gave them to Miss Gimlet for her meeting with Baldo and Councillor Daley?"

Twitch, twitch, crunch.

"You've got it. Foggy, Foggy, Foggy!"

As he walked to school, Foggy had been thinking long and hard about tactics. The way he saw it, he had three "stop Edna" options:

Option 1, codenamed SNAFFLE: keep her away from the Fayre.

Advantage: She couldn't strangle anybody if she wasn't around to do it.

Disadvantage: He couldn't think of a way of stopping her turning up that wouldn't arouse her suspicions. As a result she could strangle him instead.

Option 2, codenamed BAFFLE: keep Baldo, Miss Gimlet and Councillor Daley away from the Fayre.

Advantage: It was impossible to be strangled if you didn't stick your neck out, and if the three potential victims weren't around, they couldn't.

Disadvantage: When she finds out she's been foiled, Edna might lose her temper and strangle him for a second time.

Option 3, codename RAFFLE: let them all turn up, but follow Edna around and call for help the moment she picks out her victim and slips her hands round his or her neck. Especially his, Foggy's...

Foggy had just decided that RAFFLE was a far better bet than SNAFFLE or BAFFLE when from the entrance to the White House he heard Baldo gently bellow his name.

"Fogarty!"

"Yes, Mr Baldock?"

"Come here."

Foggy followed Baldo into his room as commanded. The English teacher winced slightly as he sat down on his chair. Although his bandaged rear still looked like an over-inflated tyre, it did seem to have developed the slowest of slow punctures.

"Yes, sir?" said Foggy, wondering what was on Baldo's mind.

Baldo fixed Foggy with a piercing look. "Madame Retsmah, alias you and Miss Grice. How do you make your predictions?"

A picture of Retsmah's sharp claws flashed into Foggy's mind. He gulped. "Sort of . . . pick them out of thin air, Mr Baldock."

Baldo snorted and shook his head. "Useless. Haven't you got a crystal ball?"

Foggy wanted to say that he'd be delighted to use a crystal ball with Retsmah, and the heavier the better, but thought better of it. He settled for a simple, "No, sir."

Baldo dipped into the side drawer of his desk. When he held up a perfect, sparkling orb, Foggy thought for a moment he was seeing double. Then he realized that only one of the sparkling orbs was Baldo's head. The other was a crystal ball.

"There you go. Use that tomorrow."

"Tomorrow?"

Baldo put on his most patient look. "Tomorrow. Summer Fayre. Miss Grice and yourself are running a stall. 'Madame Retsmah – Personal Consultations'. Far corner of the field, by the groundsman's shed. OK?"

Panic struck Foggy. "I ... we ... since when?"

"Since Miss Gimlet, dear Councillor Daley, and myself decided it at our Summer Fayre meeting yesterday."

Suddenly, Foggy's panic subsided. It was a gift from heaven. He could forget SNAFFLE and BAFFLE – even RAFFLE. If he told Edna that Baldo had decided she had to dress up as Madame Retsmah and sit in a booth all afternoon, she'd be stuck. She wouldn't be able to get out and strangle anyone!

"No problem, Mr Baldock. Leave it to us!"

Foggy almost sprinted out of Baldo's office. As he left, Baldo did something he'd never done before in his history of meetings with Foggy.

He smiled.

"Edna Grice! In my office if you please!"

Edna, arriving in school five minutes after Foggy, had heard Miss Gimlet's screech as she'd been hurrying past the White House on the way to registration.

Now, as she stood nervously before Miss Gimlet's desk, Edna wondered what was about to befall her. The answer was ... nothing.

Miss Gimlet smiled. True, it looked like the silver lining on a particularly thunderous cloud, but a smile it was.

"Edna. The Summer Fayre. How would you like to transfer your Madame Retsmah activities from the printed page to the world of one-to-one consultations?"

Edna pursed her lips. She shrugged. What on earth was the woman talking about?

Taking the silence as indecision, Miss Gimlet tried a little harder.

"There will be a booth, situated adjacent to the groundsman's shed. I thought yourself and Fogarty might like to transform it into Madame Retsmah's Fortune-Telling Emporium. Does she read palms?"

Edna shook her head. "Cards. She's from the desert. She's never seen a tree."

But, slowly, Miss Gimlet's proposal had sunk in. Edna checked to be sure. "You mean, you want us to set up our own stall thingy? For the afternoon? The *whole* afternoon?"

Miss Gimlet nodded and sighed with relief at the same time.

For her part, Edna almost did handsprings. Brilliant! She'd been racking her brains to think of a way of keeping her eyes on fearsome Foggy for the whole of the Summer Fayre, and here the answer was.

All she had to do was to tell Foggy that Miss Gimlet wanted him to dress up as Madame Retsmah and sit in their booth all afternoon and he wouldn't be able to go off and strangle anyone, anywhere!

"Leave it to us, Miss Gimlet!"

As Edna left excitedly, the headteacher sat back and watched the door rocking on its hinges. Across her thin lips flitted her second smile in as many minutes. It was a record.

Another record was about to be broken. Never in the history of Lord Turnpike School had anybody said that they *wanted* to see either Foggy or Edna.

But as Edna raced from Miss Gimlet's office and, at the same instant, Foggy darted out from Baldo's room, Councillor Daley said just that.

"How fortunate! Just the two young people I wanted to bump into! What would you both say to the idea of Madame Retsmah having her own booth at the Summer Fayre?"

Foggy shot a suspicious look at Edna. Edna fired an even more suspicious look at Foggy.

"Great!" began Foggy, thinking that if he volunteered Edna now, she'd never be able to get out of it. But no sooner had he got the first word out than Edna interrupted.

"Fab!" she cried. But before she could volunteer Foggy, Councillor Daley was in full flow again.

"Excellent! I'm delighted you agree. There will be a booth specially set up for you over by the groundsman's shed. And I've brought some wonderful costumes in with me. Just a few bits and pieces my dramatic society no longer uses, but I'm sure you'll both find something that fits."

"Both?" said Edna, looking at Foggy. "Him *and* me?"

"Like ... both?" said Foggy, looking at Edna. "Her *and* me?"

"Yes, both of you!" said Councillor Daley. "You can take turns. That way there'll always be somebody on guard ... I mean, on duty."

Foggy reflected on this. Yes, there were advantages. If he was dressed up he'd be on the spot, and not have to hide behind a tree to make sure Edna didn't nip out.

"Fine," he said.

"Finer," said Edna, who'd just come to exactly the same conclusion.

Councillor Daley watched Foggy and Edna head off to their classes. As she did so, the sunflowers on her hat began to shake. The gladioli gambolled. The dahlias danced. For, beneath them all, Councillor Daley was not merely smiling.

She was laughing.

★ ★ ★

Back home that evening, Foggy tried on the outfit he'd been given by Councillor Daley. Looking at himself in the mirror, he shuddered.

The red blouse was decidedly baggy.

The patterned headscarf would have suited a witch.

The skirt was definitely not his colour at all.

And as for the droopy gold earrings . . .

Edna's outfit was very similar, as if Councillor Daley's amateur theatrical group had bought a job lot of fortune-teller's costumes at a bazaar.

"What do you think, Retsmah?" she said to her snoozing pet. The scorpion showed no reaction one way or the other.

"OK, so it's not brilliant. But if it helps us keep an eye on Foggy then it'll be worth it. I mean, we can't just let him go around strangling people, can we? It's not fair. We've got to stop him."

Retsmah gave her a quizzical twitch, as if to say: "We? What do you mean, we?"

Edna bent low to press her nose against the glass of the scorpion's tank.

"Yes, I do mean 'we', Retsmah. I'm taking you with me. If Foggy turns nasty I'm going to need all the help I can get!"

Chapter 9

Foggy fluffed up his blouse, adjusted his scarf, hitched up his skirt, checked his earrings and stepped outside into the warm Summer Fayre air.

He felt a complete noodle.

There was only one consolation. Edna Grice looked an even bigger noodle.

She was sitting in a deckchair she'd positioned under a clutch of trees opposite their booth, a small cardboard box on her lap. Neither the deckchair nor the box were factors in her off-the-scale noodle rating, however. This was entirely due to the fact that, in addition to her Councillor Daley-supplied blouse, scarf, skirt and dangly earrings, Edna had seen fit to add a pair of motorcycle gauntlets and knee-high studded leather boots. She looked like a Hell's Fortune Teller.

"What's with the gauntlets and boots?" asked Foggy, a little worried. It had just occurred to him that in the event of some rough stuff, those boots could be very handy – or should that be footy? Painful, anyway.

Edna gave him a suspicious look. It had just occurred to her that Foggy's outfit was a perfect disguise. Dressed as he was, he'd be able to get within strangling distance of his intended victim without them having the foggiest idea it was Foggy.

"They're to keep out the cold," lied Edna, pulling the cardboard box a little closer.

Foggy looked up at the sun, shining down from a clear blue sky. Keep out the cold! A likely story! She was up to something, no doubt about it.

"You want to go on duty first?" asked Edna.

Do I? Foggy asked himself. Was she testing him with a trick question? Whoever was on fortune-telling duty would be inside the booth. The other would be outside, and able to keep an eye on everything. Where would Edna be most likely to strike – inside, or outside?

Inside, of course. The moment Baldo or Miss Gimlet or Councillor Daley turned up to have their fortunes told, those cold fingers would go to work. And the gauntlets must be to avoid leaving fingerprints on their throats! They had to be warned off!

"No, you can," said Foggy. "I'll be out here ... er ... drumming up business."

Edna thought this over. What was he up to? Inside the booth was definitely the best place to do his dirty deeds. Why did he want to take the second shift?

Because her being there had scotched his plans, of course! He needed time to think of another plan. Well that was fine – because by the time he'd done that her secret weapon would be in place.

"Okey-dokey," said Edna brightly. "See you in an hour."

As Edna disappeared, cardboard box and all, into the darkened booth, Foggy walked thoughtfully across to Edna's deckchair and sat down.

This would be the easy bit. All he had to do now was watch out for Baldo, Miss Gimlet and Councillor Daley and make sure none of them went in that booth.

A tannoy announcement told him that the Fayre had been officially opened. As usual, Councillor Daley had performed the ceremony, with Miss Gimlet close at hand. They would probably be occupied for a little while.

So, figured Foggy, the likeliest first victim would be Baldo.

He was absolutely right.

For three-quarters of an hour, a steady stream of assorted customers had visited Edna inside Madame Retsmah's booth. Under Foggy's watchful gaze, each had emerged a minute or two later laughing their socks off.

That was when Foggy saw Baldo approaching. The odd thing was, though, that he didn't appear to be heading for the booth. Rather, he was skirting through the trees and round behind it.

He's embarrassed, decided Foggy with a smile. All that "touch wood" business. Baldo was as superstitious as the rest of them, but he clearly didn't want anybody to know it. That's why he was creeping about. He didn't want to be seen going into Madame Retsmah's booth.

Leaping from the deckchair, Foggy

ducked into the trees himself. It was time for action. Not wanting to be seen going in was one thing, but if Edna had her way Baldo would never be seen coming out either.

Not that the English teacher looked to be in any hurry to go in. He'd tucked himself down by the side of the groundsman's shed and was peering out. Making certain that he wasn't going to be spotted, decided Foggy.

He crept closer. And, as he did, so crept equally close the question of exactly what he was going to say to Baldo when he reached him. A possible conversation trickled through his mind:

"Excuse me, Mr Baldock. Don't go in that booth."

"Why ever not, Fogarty?"

"Because Edna Grice is in there, waiting for you."

"I know. She'll be quite choked if I don't pay her a visit."

"You'll be very choked if you do, sir.

She's going to strangle you!"

"Don't be stupid, boy. She's going to tell me my future."

"If you go in there, you won't have a future!"

"Nonsense, Fogarty. I'm going in. . ."

Talk about a tricky one! As Foggy crept up behind Baldo he came to the conclusion that making him believe he was in mortal danger was going to be next to impossible. He'd have to think of another way.

Of course! The crystal ball in his pocket! Foggy lifted it out. Maybe he could gaze into it and predict something that would dissuade Baldo from going near that booth? Or maybe there was another way? Yes, he realized. There was.

The crystal ball cracked against Baldo's head like a well-placed snooker shot. The teacher moaned. He half-turned, his eyes glazing over even as he looked at the wild woman who'd just belted him on the bonce.

And then he began to topple.

For an uncoordinated and accident-prone article, as Baldo had described him regularly over the years, Foggy acted remarkably quickly. Grabbing the handles of the groundsman's wheelbarrow, he slid it into position just as Baldo keeled over. The teacher landed in it gracefully.

Now what? He could hardly wheel him out of the front gates and all the way home. As he leant against the wooden shed to think, inspiration struck. He would store him! Opening the shed's solid door, Foggy wheeled Baldo round and straight inside.

"Safe and sound!" he murmured, only to add, "So long as he doesn't come round."

That problem was quickly dealt with. Grabbing a ball of rough twine, more commonly used for marking cricket pitches than for tying up teachers, Foggy bound Baldo hand and foot, joining him to the wheelbarrow for good measure.

"He'll thank me later," said Foggy as he closed the hut door and headed back to the deckchair.

Inside the booth for the past hour, Edna had been busy. Before her first customer had ever arrived, she'd quickly made preparations.

Putting the cardboard box in the corner of the booth, she'd covered it with the loose folds of the canvas walls. Inside, she heard Retsmah give a gentle scratch.

"Now don't forget what I told you, Retsmah. If I get any nonsense from Foggy, I'll be over here like a flash to let you out. What you do to him after that is up to you!"

She'd checked that her boots were tightly laced, and that her gauntlets fitted snugly. A marauding scorpion wasn't going to worry her.

After that she'd settled down to her hour of fortune-telling. This had exercised Edna's mind somewhat. Keeping Retsmah under wraps as her secret weapon meant that the flash card technique wasn't on. She'd had to think of something different, yet simple.

Her solution had been just that. It employed a dice and a simple list of predictions.

1. You will get married in the Autumn
2. You will play for Manchester United one day
3. You will soon move house
4. You will have a baby next year
5. You will make a pop record
6. You will pass all your exams

As customers had arrived she'd simply tossed the dice and read out the appropriate line from her list – hence the 83-year-old grandfather Foggy had seen laughing uncontrollably after he'd been told he'd be having a baby next year.

So the system had its flaws, but it had seen her through the hour. Now, as she came out of the booth and in to the sunlight, she saw Foggy sitting in the deckchair, whistling.

"All quiet?" she asked.

Foggy thought of Baldo, safely trussed up. "Couldn't be quieter."

"In you go, then. See you in an hour."

As Foggy vanished into the booth, Edna looked around. If she was going to keep Baldo, Miss Gimlet and Councillor Daley out of frightful Foggy's clutches she was going to have to spot them in good time.

And spot Miss Gimlet in good time was exactly what she did.

It happened almost fifty minutes into Foggy's hour of duty. In that time various customers had entered and left the booth, all looking furious.

Now, as Edna peered out from the depths of the deckchair, she saw Miss Gimlet sidling through the trees and round near the big wooden shed that the groundsman stored his tools in.

The headteacher appeared to have been touring the stalls. At least, thought Edna, that's what it looked like. In her hands she was carrying a reel of sticky tape. Sticky tape? If she went into that booth Foggy wouldn't need to worry about her crying out. Miss Gimlet could be silenced with her own purchase. Talk about a bad bargain!

Swiftly Edna hurried through the trees. As she appeared on one side of the grounds-man's shed, Miss Gimlet was furtively peering round the other from behind the massive roller used for flattening the school cricket pitch.

What should she say? How could she raise the subject? Edna was in a complete quandary. Which went a long way towards explaining why, as she crept up behind Miss Gimlet, Edna ended up saying the first thing that came into her head.

"Boo!"

Startled, Miss Gimlet whirled round and

stood up in the same movement, cracking her head on the handle of the cricket pitch roller as she did so. Moments later she was lying in a crumpled heap at Edna's feet.

"Now what do I do?" Edna sighed.

It was a good question. Should she run for help? Edna rejected the thought. She couldn't afford to be away from mad and murderous Foggy for any time at all. Miss Gimlet might be no longer in any condition to enter his lair, but that still left Baldo and Councillor Daley at his mercy.

Even worse, while she was away Miss Gimlet might revive sufficiently to go into the Madame Retsmah booth for a quick reading of the bump now springing up from her head.

No, decided Edna, she couldn't take that chance. Spotting the reel of sticky tape on the ground she had an idea. How about if she was to tie Miss Gimlet up with it – loosely, of course. Then, even if she did wake up, she wouldn't be able to walk blindly into Foggy's eager hands.

Congratulating herself on the solution, Edna bound Miss Gimlet hand and foot. She'd surely appreciate why it had been necessary when Edna came and set her free at the end of the afternoon.

A nasty thought then crossed her mind. In crime programmes on telly she'd seen people tied up and left for years. It hadn't done them any good at all. They'd ended up frozen. Was it possible that Miss Gimlet could freeze to death in an afternoon?

She wouldn't have thought so. Still, better to be safe than sorry – and the solution was right on her doorstep, so to speak. All she had to do was pop her in the groundsman's shed! Nice and cosy in there!

And so, scooping the lifeless headteacher up in her arms, Edna carried her through the shed door, dodged quickly round the laden wheelbarrow the silly groundsman had left in the middle of the floor, dropped her gently in a battered old armchair, and hurried out again.

Foiled you, Foggy!

Foggy looked at the spotty individual sitting on the other side of the table, then down into his crystal ball.

"My psychic powers tell me," he droned, "that you are in Year 9 at Lord Turnpike School. Am I right?"

"Of course you're right, bonehead," snapped the spotty individual. "I'm in the same Maths group as you. I want to know what next year holds for me."

Foggy stared intently into the crystal ball. "A-ha. The mists are clearing. Yes, yes . . . I predict, with the utmost confidence . . ."

"What?"

"That next year. . ."

"Yes? Tell me!"

"You will be in Year 10. . ."

As the spotty individual stormed out in disgust, Foggy checked his watch. His hour was up. Time to get Edna the Executioner back in the booth and under his watchful eye. He stood up and peered outside.

She wasn't there! The deck-chair was an Edna-free zone. Foggy's eyes narrowed grimly. So where was she?

He edged round the rear side of the booth to see how the land lay. And it lay, he saw immediately, very badly!

Beyond the groundsman's shed – the shed in which Baldo had been safely stored and preserved from Edna's clutches – he could see the gruesome girl herself, peeking suspiciously out from behind the cricket pitch roller.

And who was she peeking suspiciously out at? None other than Councillor Daley, who was herself peeking suspiciously *into* the groundsman's hut!

Both she and Baldo were at Edna's mercy! There was no time to lose!

Hitching up his skirt, Foggy began sprinting for all he was worth.

Behind the roller, Edna had seen enough. After safely depositing Miss Gimlet in the shed, she'd been on the way back to her deckchair when she'd seen Councillor Daley tip-toeing through the trees.

At that moment she'd decided to tell Councillor Daley what was going on and enlist her help. Exactly how to explain it all hadn't been so easy to work out, though, so she'd taken refuge behind the roller while she thought about what to say.

Then, sensing that Councillor Daley had actually come closer she'd peeped out to check. And what had she seen? The councillor looking through the shed window – and, gazing wickedly round the side of the booth like the **Big Bad Wolf** sizing up little

Red Robin Hood – Foggy the Frightful!

The strangler was preparing to strike! She had to act!

Leaping out from behind the roller, Edna began to sprint.

And so it was, that at the instant Councillor Daley put her shoulder to the door of the groundsman's shed and burst angrily inside, so Foggy and Edna arrived from opposite sides to burst in on her.

Chapter 10

They were met by the most amazing sight.

Edna, the words "Leave her be, Foggy, you black-hearted stinkeroo!" on her lips, suddenly found herself incapable of uttering a word.

Foggy, poised to cry "Hands off, Edna Grice, you blood-thirsty throttler!" found himself unable to manage a sound.

Screeching to a halt, the best that both of them could do was stand and stare.

For, having burst through the door like a marauding tank, Councillor Daley hadn't left it at that. She'd gripped the wheelbarrow by its handles, tipped Baldo out, and was now in the process of trying to – there was no other word for it – *strangle* him!

Baldo, for his part, clearly had plans of his own. Even with Councillor Daley on the attack, he'd managed to rip himself free of the garden twine Foggy had used to tie him up. The struggle had brought him within striking distance of Miss Gimlet, and it was an opportunity he'd obviously grabbed with both hands, since they were round Miss Gimlet's neck. He was strangling her!

And Miss Gimlet? Twisting free from the loops of sticky tape Edna had used on her, the headteacher fought back with a vengeance. But not by trying to fight off Baldo. Instead, she threw herself on the councillor and – Foggy and Edna were totally agreed on this point – started to strangle *her*.

"What's going on?" yelled Edna.

"They're ... they're strangling each other," said Foggy, confused.

"Just like Retsmah's prediction," gasped Edna.

Foggy stared at her. "But I thought *you* were going to be doing that."

"Me?" Edna gawped at Foggy. "I thought it was going to be *you!*"

They both turned back to the three-way battle going on before them.

"But it's *them*," said Foggy. "Why?"

Edna shrugged. "I don't know. Maybe it's one of those, y'know, what we do in Geometry – Equilateral Tri-strangles."

Foggy didn't even try to work out what she could be referring to. All he knew was what he could see – that Councillor Daley was throttling Baldo, Baldo was trying to twist Miss Gimlet's head off and Miss Gimlet was doing her best to tie a knot in Councillor Daley's neck.

"Stop!" he yelled. "Mr Baldock! Miss Gimlet! Councillor Daley! Stop!"

The three stranglers took no notice.

"You're all being very silly," cried Edna. "All three of you. If you don't stop at once I'll report you to Miss Gimlet on Monday!"

The three strangled on, especially Miss Gimlet, who clearly wasn't worried at the prospect of being reported to herself.

Foggy could think of only one other course of action. "Edna," he yelled. "Let's go get the Police Marching Band to help!"

It did the trick. Without knowing why, Foggy had managed to strike a chord.

"Not necessary, Fogarty," said Baldo, immediately letting go of Miss Gimlet's neck.

"Indeed. All over now," said Miss Gimlet, simultaneously removing her hands from Councillor Daley's throat.

"Quite so. Storm in a tea-cup," said Councillor Daley, releasing the stranglehold she had on Baldo.

Breathing heavily, the three backed warily away from each other.

"Now do you believe Retsmah's a star?" Edna asked Foggy. "She predicted it all!"

"Tosh. Complete and utter rubbish."

Edna glared indignantly at the source of the insult. "I beg your pardon, Mr Baldock?"

"Total claptrap," growled Baldo. "You had 'stranger' in your computer file. It was *me* who changed it to 'strangler'."

"You!" said Foggy. "But why?"

"Same reason I planted the flowers and slopped my best brandy in a flask of soup," snapped Baldo. "Because I wanted a certain somebody out of the way. I wanted her to think her horoscope was going to come true again."

Miss Gimlet gasped. "You? You did those things?"

"Too right," said Baldo. "But the flowers weren't strong enough to lay you out, were they? Nor was the brandy I slipped in your soup. I was a mug. I should have done it the other way round and slipped soup in the brandy."

"But – why?" stammered Miss Gimlet.

"Because with you out of the way it would mean sharing the money between just two of us instead of three," he snapped. "Between Jemimah and I."

He gazed adoringly at Councillor Daley, his head blushing all over so that he looked like a ripe plum. "I love you, Jemimah. I want to run off with you to a tropical island and spend the rest of my life with you beneath swaying palms laden with ripe coconuts."

"Ahhh," cooed Edna. "How romantic."

Councillor Jemimah Daley, however, was not of the same opinion.

"Coconuts!" she scoffed. "The only one who's nuts round here, Baldo, is you! I wouldn't be seen dead on a beach with you!"

"Bang goes the romance," whispered Foggy.

"Who do you think changed that 'flower' prediction to 'flour'?" snarled Councillor Daley. "Me, of course! I put that flour bomb in position. And if it hadn't caught on that picture of Lord Turnpike you wouldn't have known what had hit you! The same goes for the encyclopaedia. Bad luck again. If that had hit you on the head instead of where you keep your brains, you'd have been out of action good and proper!"

"But ... why?" said a shocked Baldo.

"Why else? With you out of the way, *I* could share the money with my *sister*!"

"Councillor Daley – Miss Gimlet – they're ... sisters?" asked Foggy.

"Looks like it," nodded Edna.

"It *is* like it," confirmed Councillor Daley. "Before my ill-fated and thankfully short marriage to Ebenezer Daley, my name was Jemimah Gimlet."

The councillor, businesswoman, and Chair of Governors moved across to Miss

Gimlet and looped a flabby arm round the headteacher's shoulders. "Share and share alike. Just like we always have."

"Share!" screeched Miss Gimlet. "You wanted to share the money with me?"

Shrugging off the flabby arm, Miss Gimlet swung round on her sister, eyes blazing. "Steal it from me, you mean! You've never shared anything with me in your whole life, Jemimah. I never even got your old clothes!"

"Only because they'd have drowned you, dear."

It wasn't an argument that seemed to impress Miss Gimlet. The headteacher laughed coldly.

"Who do you think changed that 'letter' prediction? Who do you think let that bee loose at the sewage farm? Me, of course! I couldn't think of any better way of getting rid of you than by having you drown in a tank of smelly sludge, you ... you stinker!"

"Mildred!"

Miss Gimlet was in full flow now. "Don't Mildred me! Who do you think pruned your stupid hat? Me. I wanted you to think your horoscopes were coming true so that you would be too frightened to turn up today. I wanted *you* out of the way, Jemimah!"

"Why? Why, Mildred?"

"So that I could take your share of the money of course! Take it and run off to a warm, tropical island with the only man I've ever loved!"

"And who's that?" screeched Councillor Daley.

Miss Gimlet turned tenderly and tearfully towards Baldo. "With you, you flower-sending, soup-spiking swine!"

Foggy's head was swimming. "Oh, good grief! What *is* going on?"

Edna sighed. "Foggy, haven't you been listening? Baldo wants to share the money with Councillor Daley because he loves her, but she doesn't love him because she's best friends with her sister Miss Gimlet, and that's who she wants to share the money with, but the trouble is Miss Gimlet isn't best friends with her because she wants to share the money with the love of her life who is Baldo, but then we come back to the start again because Baldo doesn't love her, he loves Councillor Daley and wants to share the money with her. Got it?"

"Er . . . I think so," muttered Foggy.

"Sounded a remarkably clear explanation to me," said Baldo. "Most uncharacteristic."

"Amazingly clear," said Miss Gimlet. "The girl has got hidden talents."

"A credit to the school," said Councillor Daley. "If not to her teachers."

Foggy nodded. "Couldn't agree more. Crystal clear, Edna. Except for one thing."

"Which is?" sighed Edna.

"What money?"

The effect of the question was dramatic.

Baldo, Miss Gimlet and Councillor Daley immediately looked at each other.

"The money," hissed Councillor Daley. "How could we have lost sight of that? We've all been very silly. In spite of our differences we can still share out the money."

Baldo nodded, the memory of the councillor's attacks on him clearly forgotten. "You're right, Jemimah. One third is nearly the same as one half."

A fleeting smile crossed Miss Gimlet's face, a sure sign that Baldo's soup sabotage had been forgiven. "Once we've *got* the money, that is."

Councillor Daley rubbed her hands together, her sister's attempt to send her through the county's sewage system accepted as one of those little spats that sisters have now and again. "Which is going to be no problem," she gloated. "Because our plan to steal it is fool-proof."

"There you go, Foggy," said Edna

brightly, "that's what money – the money they're going to steal..."

"With their fool-proof plan..." said Foggy.

They looked at each other.

They looked at Councillor Daley, Miss Gimlet and Baldo.

They looked done for.

"Grab 'em!" screeched Miss Gimlet.

As Baldo seized Foggy, Councillor Daley grabbed Edna. Within seconds they were both bound hands and feet, Foggy with the garden twine he'd used on Baldo and Edna with a large quantity of Miss Gimlet's sticky tape.

"Shall I do something serious to them as well?" asked Baldo, an evil glint in his eye. "To stop them raising the alarm?"

"They won't be found until Monday," said Councillor Daley. "By then we'll be miles away."

"But I *want* to do something serious to them," pleaded Baldo. "I've wanted to do something serious to them for ages and ages."

"No," said Miss Gimlet. "Just gag them. We've wasted enough time as it is."

"What are you goging do boo?" Foggy's question was interrupted by a lump of smelly rag being wrapped round his mouth by Baldo.

"What are we going to do?" growled the English teacher. "Swipe that million pounds, of course. Why do think we worked so hard to get it on display? We've been planning this all year."

"What you wodda goo bat gor?" asked Edna as she, too, had a gag put over her mouth.

Miss Gimlet bent low. "What do we want to do that for, Miss Grice? For my part, I would have thought the answer to that was obvious. To get me out of this school! Out of teaching! Away from cretins like you and Fogarty for ever!"

"You and me both," Baldo laughed hysterically.

"And out of business for me," said Councillor Daley. "A printing business that's about to go bust, unfortunately. There are going to be a lot of people after me next week. But with my share of that million I'm going to be on the other side of the world by then!"

Miss Gimlet was already at the shed door and pointing to her watch. "Come on. It's nearly four-thirty."

Baldo hurried to join her, pausing only to turn to Foggy and Edna. "Looks like you two will have an exclusive for the next *Term Times*," he laughed. "Tell you what, I'll even give you a headline. 'Terrific trio carry out audacious robbery.' How's that?"

Miss Gimlet cackled. "One million pounds swiped as police march away!"

"Madame Retsmah fails to predict it!"

hooted Councillor Daley, joining them at the shed door.

"Gow goo goiging go goo ig?" cried Foggy.

"How are we going to do it?" interpreted Baldo. "That has to be the most sensible question you've ever asked in your life, Fogarty. So it deserves a good answer. We're going to do it thanks to your help!"

"Let me tell them," said Miss Gimlet. "My office used to be Lord Turnpike's bedroom. I was spring-cleaning a little while ago and guess what I found? A map. A map of the loopy Lord's tunnel-digging plans."

"So we went out and did some digging around ourselves," grinned Councillor Daley. "And the plan was accurate. Under some undergrowth we found the entrance to the very tunnel Lord Turnpike got lost in!"

"That was when we came up with our master plan," Baldo said smugly. "Get a million pound display for the Summer

Fayre. Make sure it's sited at one end of the tunnel. Then, while it's being guarded from the front, nip up from the other end of the tunnel and snaffle it!"

"Goo bon't ged abay wid id!" bellowed Edna through her gag.

"Oh, but we will get away with it," said Miss Gimlet, "because we won't be seen on the scene. Most of the guards are members of the Police Marching Band, you see. And those that aren't will be watching the display – which starts –" she checked her watch again – "in precisely three minutes!"

"Time we had our fortunes told, then," laughed Councillor Daley. Her chins wobbled as she pointed at Foggy and Edna. "A clever touch that, don't you think? Having the tunnel which leads to our fortune being safely hidden by a fortune-telling booth?"

Fortune-telling booth. Madame Retsmah's booth? Foggy's eyes asked the question. It had to, his mouth couldn't.

"Yes, that's how you've been helping us all afternoon, Fogarty," crowed Baldo. "That's why we asked you to do your Madame Retsmah act. We couldn't take the chance of the entrance to our tunnel being accidentally discovered by a wandering visitor. Putting that booth above it, and having you two guard it all afternoon, was the perfect solution!"

Miss Gimlet positively beamed. "Our master-stroke. The guarantee that we'll be given maximum getaway time."

"Ghat?" said Edna.

"Gow?" said Foggy.

"Because when the marching band finish and they discover that tunnel, you two will be the prime suspects," said Councillor Daley.

"The police will interrogate you both," said Miss Gimlet. "They will try to get some sensible answers."

Baldo came in with the coup-de-grace.

"And as none of us have managed that in all the time you pair have been here, we're pretty sure the police won't have any more success. By the time you've driven them round the bend we'll be miles away!"

Miss Gimlet tapped her watch sharply.

Baldo nodded.

Councillor Daley yanked open the shed door.

Out they went, still laughing. Bound and gagged, Foggy and Edna could only watch them through the murky window as they scurried across to the deserted fortune-telling booth and disappeared inside...

Chapter 11

They headed straight for the small round table at which Foggy and Edna had been sitting for their consultations.

With a chuckle, Miss Gimlet swept the crystal ball off the green baize cloth and sent it rolling into the corner of the booth.

With a chortle, Councillor Daley grabbed hold of the table and tossed it aside.

With a chisel, Baldo bent down and began prising up the grass that had been covered over by the table. Beneath it lay a solid square wooden board. The English teacher levered that up too, to reveal nothing but the gaping hole that was the entrance to Lord Turnpike's tunnel.

"OK," snapped Baldo. "I'll go down, grab the money and bring it back. You two wait here."

A bony hand landed on his shoulder. Miss Gimlet was no longer chuckling.

"After your performance lately? I wouldn't trust you as far as I could throw you. You could have discovered another way out for all I know."

"I haven't, I promise. I'll turn round and come straight back. Don't you believe me?"

"No," said Miss Gimlet. "Which is why I'm coming too. I'm going to be right behind you."

"In which case," snarled Councillor Daley, no longer chortling, "*I* will be right behind *you*, baby sister, because I wouldn't trust you any further than I could throw you ... or do I mean any further than you could throw me? Whatever, I don't trust you. So there."

"All three of us can't go down," said Baldo.

"All three of us *can* go down," said Miss Gimlet.

"And *are* going down," snapped Councillor Daley. "So get moving."

With a sigh, Baldo eased himself down into the hole.

Behind him, Miss Gimlet briefly dangled her legs over the edge before letting herself down too.

Councillor Daley followed. A deep breath, a mighty squeeze, and then she was through the hole and down into the tunnel as well.

Off they went, heading for the fortune at the other end...

Back in the groundsman's shed, Foggy and Edna both had a clear picture of what should happen now.

Foggy could see that he should fight and kick his way across to the pair of garden shears he could see. He should lever them open with his knees, then turn round and use them to saw through the twine tying his hands together.

Then he should release Edna and, together, they should rush across and raise the alarm.

For her part, Edna could see that she should think of a brilliantly brilliant way of bursting free from the bands of sticky tape that had been wound round her.

Maybe by imagining she was a Christmas present and seeing if that helped her fight her way free?

Or, more likely, by fighting and kicking her way across to the lawnmower she could see, and using the blades to saw through the sticky tape tying her hands together.

After that she could release Foggy and,

together, they could rush across and raise the alarm!

That was what they knew should happen next.

What a pain, thought Foggy. *If only those shears weren't sitting on that shelf where I can't reach them.*

It's really, really unfair, thought Edna. *If only that wasn't an electric lawnmower.*

And so they were both still completely unable to move as, in the distance, they heard the sound of the Police Marching Band strike up.

It was a sound that Baldo, Miss Gimlet and Councillor Daley heard with some pleasure as they reached the end of the tunnel. If the next part of their plan proceeded as smoothly as the rest of it they would soon be a million pounds better off.

Reaching up, Baldo slid back the wooden panel that led up to the spot immediately behind the table upon which all that delicious dosh was being displayed.

Councillor Daley gave Miss Gimlet a leg up. The headteacher popped her head over the edge, then straight back down again.

"Perfect!" she whispered. "Only two police on guard. And they're facing the other way, watching the marchers!"

"What're you waiting for, then?" hissed her sister. "Go get it."

With Baldo and Councillor Daley taking a leg each, Miss Gimlet was boosted high enough out of the tunnel to attach a large wodge of her sticky tape to the back of the glass money cabinet.

Moments later she'd silently reeled it off the table and into her gleeful arms.

Moments after that she was let back down into the tunnel and into the gleeful arms of Baldo and Councillor Daley.

And moments after that, with the trapdoor back in place, the three crooks were retracing their steps towards the tunnel's entrance and their escape through Madame Retsmah's booth to lives of luxury and leisure.

Behind them, the band played on.

It was twenty minutes later, at five o'clock precisely, that two things came off together.

The first was the Police Marching Band, by the exit at the far end of the main arena.

The second was Edna's sticky tape gag, by accident.

Wondering how long it would be before they were found, and concerned that she might starve to death in the meantime, Edna had racked her brains about possible sources of nourishment.

Concluding that, under the circumstances, the only thing available to her was the sticky tape covering her mouth, she'd started licking it – only to discover that wet sticky tape quickly loses its stick.

After that, events moved quickly. A few

minutes of chewing and spitting saw the twine round Foggy's hands torn away.

Quickly Foggy undid the rest of his bindings, then set about releasing Edna.

"Now what?" said Foggy. "Run and get the police?"

"Ooh, I don't know," said Edna, uncertainly. "What if they *do* think it's us who's nabbed that money? I don't want to be locked up, Foggy. It'll be horrible. Jails are full of bars and I don't like the smell of beer."

Foggy hesitated. Edna's logic apart, the girl had a point. Baldo had said they'd be the first suspects, and he was probably right.

"Maybe they didn't manage to steal that money," he said hopefully.

A piercing shriek of a police whistle from the direction of the main arena put paid to that hope.

"The missing million! It must have been discovered!" cried Edna.

"Edna, you can't discover something that's missing. It's either there, in which case you can discover it, or it's not – in which case. . ."

"In which case we'd better run for it!" said Edna. "I'm going home!"

Yanking open the shed door, she began to hare away – only to stop and hare back again.

"Where are you going?"

"The booth!" shouted Edna.

"We don't want to go in there! If we're found in there when the police come. . ."

"I've got to go in that booth! I've got to!"

As she raced away, Foggy followed.

"Don't! You'll leave forensic evidence!"

He galloped across the turf. Ahead of him, Edna was already pulling aside the booth's canvas flap.

"They'll be able to prove we've been in there!" he yelled as he reached the booth and ploughed inside after Edna. "They'll think the crime was committed by us. They'll think we're really. . ."

The words dried on his lips as he took in the scene before him.

Edna was stock still, her eyes wide and staring.

She was staring at the hole in the floor out of which three heads protruded – the heads of Baldo, Miss Gimlet and Councillor Daley.

Petrified, unable to go back down the tunnel or get out the way they'd come, they were staring too. . .

. . . At the small, brown and very, very nasty-looking scorpion that had been let out of its cardboard box by the crystal ball that Baldo had tossed aside.

"Madame Retsmah!" breathed Foggy, finally managing to complete his sentence.

"Standing guard!" said Edna.

"Take it away!" screamed Baldo, Miss Gimlet and Councillor Daley together.

Edna picked up her leather gauntlets, still

in the booth where she'd left them. Putting them on, she scooped Retsmah into her hands and carried her nearer the three crooks.

"Foggy, go get the police," she said. "I'll stay here with Retsmah and look after these three until her prediction for them comes true."

"Comes true? The strangling, you mean?"

Edna's pealing laugh bounced off the walls of the booth.

"No, the other bit. 'Unlucky day, Saturday,' remember! I told you she could tell the future, didn't I!"

Edna and Foggy sat reading the *Term Times* front page. It didn't matter that it had been typed up in something of a hurry, and that Edna's keyboarding had suffered badly as a result.

It was *their* front page.

It was *their* story!

TERRIBLE TREE-O CURRY OUT AUDACIOUS RUBBERY

Pillion mounds swiped from under the hoses of the polite mooching band

MADAME RETSMAH SAVES IT!

Inclusive report
by
Enda Groce and James Fogeytree

An attempted slobbery was fooled on Raturday at the Summer Fayre.

Three crocks, better known to all at the school as Claude 'Blado' Bladock (52), Ms Grimlet (56), and Countskewer Jemimah Daley (53), used Lord Tornpuke's secret tunnel to get at the £1 million on display.

After tying up your intrepid reporters in the groundsman's sled, they went down the tunnel which was hidden from view by the Madame Retsmah's fortune-toiling bath. The other end came up underwear the money was. Snuffling it while the gourds were witching the Police Band, the three ~~boobies~~ baddies were all ready to make their getawhy.

But they failed! Little known to them, Retsmah (2) had escarpered from her glass tonk and was standing there waiting for them!

Frightened of being stunk, the three stinkers had to stew where they were until the police arrived and took them into custardy.

In recognition of their wonderful work, yours trulies, Enda and Figgy, have been mad chuff reproters for *Term Times*.

Watch this spice!

Edna looked at the piece on the screen with undisguised pride.

"What do you reckon, Foggy?"

"I'm chuffed," grinned Foggy. "It's absolunatically the best reprot you've ever triped!"